NOT ANOTHER ALPHA MALE

Not Another Romance Novel

R.L. KENDERSON

ISBN-13: 978-1-950918-46-1

Editor: Jovana Shirley, Unforeseen Editing, www.unforeseenediting.com
Cover Designer: R.L. Kenderson at R.L. Cover Designs, www.
rlcoverdesigns.com

Not Another Alpha Male

Chapter One

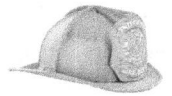

PRU

"IT'S POSITIVE."

I flew off my chair and gave my friend Alexis the tightest squeeze. I always knew deep down that she wasn't the reason she and her ex-husband hadn't had a baby. And I was right.

She had just found out she and her new husband were going to have a baby at our monthly United She-Woman Single Ladies with Our Vibrators So We Never Have Another Bad Date or Experience Romance Again Because Men Suck Club dinner.

We weren't an official club or anything. We were just a group of friends who had sworn off men—or rather, had tried to. Tessa and Alexis were married, Bree was getting married next month, and Paisley lived with her boyfriend. The only ones left were Elizabeth, Isabelle, and me, and for a while there, Isabelle had been dating someone too.

Our club wasn't so much a club anymore but an inside joke.

Except I knew that I was going to be one of the women who stayed single. Maybe twenty years from now, I'd change my mind, but I liked my freedom. I sure missed dick though. Unfortunately, that beautiful piece of pleasure was usually attached to a man.

Tessa grinned at Alexis. "You'd better call Trevor."

She grinned back, her face lit up with awe. "I think I'm going to wait until I get home."

I took a sip of my wine, thinking this was the best monthly dinner we'd had in a long time as a group when Bree had to ruin it.

She bolted upright from her chair and shouted the one name I hadn't wanted to hear.

"*Sebastian.*"

She waved her arm back and forth while I tried to make myself as small as possible.

I liked to think of myself as a strong, independent woman. But I was also a woman who didn't need any drama, and staying away from Sebastian Creed was how I had planned to accomplish that.

"Hey, coz," Bree said, giving him a hug when he reached us. "What are you doing here?"

"Getting some dinner with a couple of guys from work." Sebastian looked around, his eyes lingering on me for an extra beat before moving on. "Good evening, ladies."

Everyone smiled and said hello, except me. I understood where they were coming from. He was Bree's cousin, and he was tall, dark, and handsome. But even as sexy as he was, I wasn't going to be pulled into his allure. I gave a single wave and looked away, hoping he'd get the hint and go away.

"You're with colleagues. Are you here on business or pleasure?" Bree asked.

"A little bit of both. I'm the new guy at work, so my captain nominated me to plan the annual charity event." He smiled a fake smile. "Aren't I a lucky guy?"

"Oh my God," Bree said, and I shook my head back and forth for what it was worth. She wasn't looking at me. "Pru is an event planner. I bet she'd give you the friends and family discount."

I jumped off my chair. "No, I will not."

Sebastian eyed me and smirked. "Sounds like a plan."

"Did you hear me? I already said no."

"Come on, Pru. It's a charity event," Bree whined.

"Yeah, Pru," Paisley agreed.

They weren't going to let this go easily. I needed to come up with an excuse. "I don't even know what the event is."

"It's the Annual Golden Prairie Firefighters Charity Event. This year, we're giving the proceeds away to..." He winced. "I'll have to get back to you on that one."

I rolled my eyes. He didn't even know the charity of the event that he was supposed to plan. *Figures.*

"I've been to this event, Pru," Alexis said. "They always pick excellent charities."

I frowned. *Thanks a lot, Alexis.*

My friends didn't seem to understand that I didn't want to be around Sebastian, and to find out what he did for a living made it so much worse.

I put my hands on my hips. "Are you saying you're a firefighter?"

Sebastian held out his arms. "Guilty."

There was nothing guilty in that smile. He liked flaunting his profession.

"I don't believe you," I said just to piss him off.

He laughed in disbelief. "Bree?"

She frowned questioningly at me. "He's always been a fireman."

It was like everyone at this table was conspiring against me.

I sat down and crossed my arms and legs. Hopefully, my body language matched the next words coming out of my mouth. "I'm not doing it."

"Yes, she is," Bree told Sebastian. "I'll make sure she gets your contact info."

Unbelievable.

After Sebastian left to join his coworkers, Bree looked at me. "Why won't you do this? I bet this thing would be a walk in the park for you."

"Because I don't want to, okay?"

I didn't understand why Bree was asking. She knew I wasn't her cousin's biggest fan.

Bree put her hands up. "Fine. Don't do it then. Don't help my cousin and a charity."

I sighed. She was guilt-tripping me, and it was going to work.

"Okay, I'll do it. But I'm not charging him the friends and family discount because he is neither friend nor family. And there is no foe discount."

Isabelle started laughing as if I'd told the best joke in the world, and I couldn't help but smile.

"Foe?" Paisley asked. "Did I miss something?"

"Pru's still mad that Sebastian threw a frog at her when we were five years old," Bree said with a laugh.

"Thanks, Bree. Way to make me sound like I hold a grudge," I said.

"You do hold a grudge," she retorted.

I looked around at the rest of our friends. "The frog thing didn't help, but no, I am not still mad about that. Back when Bree went to her cousin Tina's wedding, I drove her wedding outfit up to her because she'd forgotten it."

"I helped too," Tessa quickly added.

"I was talking to Bree, thinking we were alone. I asked how things were going with her family and her fake date when Sebastian snuck behind me and listened in. He scared the shit out of me, and I accidentally elbowed him in the gut. That's how close he was to me." I made sure our friends understood. "And then he called me annoying and mean."

"Oh, please. He was joking. He just wanted to get a rise out of you."

"Well, I guess it worked."

I thought my friends would understand now that I had explained my side, but most of them were stupidly in love and didn't understand.

"It sounds like he was mad that you'd elbowed him, so he wanted to make you mad back," Isabelle said, as if two wrongs made a right.

"Because he had come up so closely behind me," I protested.

"I bet he didn't mean to scare you," Bree said, "because he knew that I knew he was coming. I think you're making it a bigger deal than it needs to be."

"You're just saying that because you're related to him."

"Oh, come on, Pru. I've talked with Sebastian before. He's a nice guy," Paisley said.

"That's what every neighbor says after they find out the guy they've been living next door to is a serial killer."

"Since Sebastian and I are the only two in Bree and Zack's bridal party, I've spent some time with him," Tessa said. "He really is a nice guy."

I picked up my purse from the floor and put it over my shoulder. "I can't with any of you."

"Pru?" Elizabeth said.

She was the only one who had not said anything in Sebastian's defense so far.

I raised my eyebrows. "What?"

"I believe everything you said, and I think you have every right to not like him."

I smiled. "Thank you, Elizabeth."

"But it's not like you have to marry the man, like Alexis

did. I still think you should plan the party because he's Bree's family."

I smashed my hands down on the table and stood. "I'm leaving before I end up wishing you all choke on your dinners."

"Pru, Pru. Come back, Pru," was all I heard as I walked away.

I wasn't really that upset, but I'd already had a long day at work, and listening to them drone on and on about how great Sebastian was had just been too much for me.

So they'd know I still loved them, I spun on my heel, blew them a kiss, and turned back around. I went in the direction Sebastian had headed until I found him.

He was sitting with two other guys who were as muscular as he was. I knew that fighting fires for a living wasn't easy and took strength, but I was tired of musclemen who thought they were God's gift to women just because they had great bodies.

When it came to sex, half of them lay there and waited for their partners to do all the work because they thought they could make women come by their looks alone. No one was that hot, but try telling them that.

The three men stopped talking when they saw me approaching.

I threw my card on the table and pushed it over to Sebastian with my forefinger.

"Just know, I'm doing this for Bree, and if you so much as flake on me even once, you're on your own. Come by my office tomorrow at nine in the morning."

Chapter Two

PRU

"PRU."

Sighing, I turned around to see that Sebastian had followed me outside the restaurant. His dark hair blew in the wind, and his brown eyes were locked on me.

I sighed. "What?"

He waved my card between his first two fingers. "I can't come to your office tomorrow at nine," he said when he reached me.

I smiled and shrugged. "Oh well. At least I tried." As I spun on my heel, my smile turned to a grin.

Until Sebastian grabbed my hand and twirled me back around. I almost bumped into him but just managed to stop short.

He clenched his jaw. "Tomorrow is Thursday. You know, most people have to work on Thursdays. You're doing this on purpose."

This close to him, I could tell how good he smelled. It made me think of getting naked.

"Pru."

Oh. I turned my head away and took a deep breath of non-Sebastian air. "Fine. Do you think you could call me at nine instead?"

He nodded. "Yes."

Dammit.

"Okay, we'll talk at nine then."

This time, when I walked away, he let me go. I hoped sometime between now and nine tomorrow morning, he'd magically lose my card.

———

I picked up fast food on the way home since I had left my friends before eating dinner. Then, I went home and sat in front of the TV while I ate dinner. I loved my friends, but I didn't mind a quiet night alone.

After I calmed down, I picked up my phone and texted my friends.

> Me: I'm sorry I overreacted and left the restaurant.

> Bree: Who is this?

> Tessa: Yeah, I don't recognize this number.

Paisley: How did you get on our message thread?

Me: I'm a shitty friend.

Bree: Oh, it's Pru.

She followed it up with a laugh emoji.

Me: I'm glad to see you're not mad.

Isabelle: Nah, we had a long talk after you left. It's okay that you left us.

Me: A long talk? About me? What did you say about me?

Elizabeth: Not about you specifically. Just about life.

Me: I don't believe a word of that.

Isabelle: LOL. But you have no choice.

Me: Hey, where's Alexis?

Paisley: She went home to tell Trevor she's pregnant. They're probably doing it right now.

Elizabeth: How is finding out you're pregnant sexy?

I shook my head and smiled. I wished Elizabeth would

just be true to herself and the rest of us. No one would judge her.

> Paisley: How can it not be?

I didn't really get how my friends could be so clueless. Elizabeth didn't look at a guy and think, *Put a baby in me*, or, *He's so hot that my ovaries exploded.* That was why she didn't understand the concept.

Unlike everyone else, I was going to have mercy on Elizabeth.

> Me: First of all, it depends on the person. Obviously, people can be ecstatic, and others can panic. And some don't want to have sex with their partner.

> Me: But there is something about knowing this hot guy that you love put a baby in you. It's like a primal thing. He's marked you forever.

> Bree: Pru, I had no idea.

> Paisley: Pru has a breeding kink.

> Me: No, I don't. BUT I can understand how people do. And I don't judge.

> Bree: Ha! You judge Sebastian, and you hardly know him.

That was because he was the kind of guy women

wanted to put babies in them. Just because he was good-looking and walked around like he had a big dick.

> Alexis: I'm here! And, no, I wasn't having sex. But I do have something to share with you.

Saved by Alexis.

I didn't want to justify my animosity toward Sebastian. A few months ago, Bree would have understood, but now, she was engaged to a former manwhore. She wouldn't get it.

The next message that came across my phone was a video from Alexis. As I hit play, I scooted down on my couch as if I were going to watch a movie or something.

The clip started with Alexis outside her door and her walking into her house. We couldn't see her, but she was obviously the one recording.

I watched as she walked into the living room, where her husband, Trevor, was lounging on the couch with a bag of chips and a cat on his lap. His eyes lit up when he saw Alexis, and my breath caught at the love in his eyes.

"How was dinner?" His gaze shifted to her hand, and he grinned. "Are those leftovers for me?"

"You can have them. I wasn't very hungry."

Trevor frowned as he moved the cat from his legs and stood. "Are you feeling okay?" he asked, taking the box of food from her and leaning forward. He disappeared from the camera as the sound of a kiss was picked up by the microphone.

They both headed for the kitchen, and the image on the camera got shaky until I realized that Alexis was propping up her phone, so she could record the two of them together.

Trevor sat at the counter and lifted the lid on the to-go box while Alexis pulled open a drawer and handed him a fork.

"Remember how I said I have a surprise for you?"

"How could I forget? That was only a few hours ago." He stabbed a piece of food and popped it into his mouth. "Are you doing something with The Purrfect Café?"

"I can see why you'd guess that, but no." Alexis smiled as she bit her lip with nervousness and reached into her pocket. She pulled out her pregnancy test and slid it over to Trevor.

His brow furrowed in confusion as he picked it up and studied it.

I could tell when he realized what he was looking at, and I almost started crying.

The expression on his face was priceless.

He slowly raised his eyes up to his wife. "Is this what I think it is?"

Alexis had already given in to her emotions and had tears flowing down her cheeks. She nodded and stepped away from the counter.

Trevor jumped out of his seat and scooped her up into his arms. She clung to him in a way that showed she loved and trusted him.

I didn't think I had ever experienced that with any man I'd ever dated.

"How did this happen?" Trevor asked when he set her down on her feet.

"Since Kevin didn't actually get Candace pregnant and my fertility studies came back fine, it was probably him that whole time we were married and trying. I hope that means you're okay with this."

Trevor cupped her face. "Alexis Nelson, I'm ecstatic."

That was where the video cut off, and I put my phone down with a sigh.

I was so happy for my friend—I was happy for all my friends—but there was a twinge of jealousy in my chest. I knew I was better off alone, but sometimes, it still hurt anyway.

Chapter Three

SEBASTIAN

I DRIED off my hair with my towel and put on my uniform. After a quick finger-comb, I picked up the card Pru had set on my dinner table last night.

PRUDENCE MAXWELL
ESSENCE EVENTS, MINNEAPOLIS, MN
EVENT AND PARTY PLANNER
651-555-9678
PRUDENCEMAXWELL@ESSENCEEVENTS.COM

It was after ten in the morning now, which probably made Pru ecstatic since I hadn't been able to call at the scheduled time. But there had been a large house fire that morning, preventing me from calling her.

I thought about just forgetting about asking her to help, but I really needed to get this charity event done right. Even though I wasn't a probationary firefighter—I had over ten years of experience—I was the new guy. I thought it almost made it worse that I was totally new to this job.

Most of my colleagues had welcomed me with open arms, but my captain was still waiting to grant me his approval. And he was the one who had assigned planning the event to me. I thought he secretly hoped I would mess it up. Or maybe I was just cynical.

"Are you going to call her?"

I looked up to see Rory standing next to me. He was one of the guys I'd gone to dinner with last night, and he didn't wait for me to answer.

Rory waved his hand. "We live in an area with over two million people. She's not the only party planner out there. Find someone else."

I snorted. As soon as I returned home last night, I had tried that but failed. Turned out, event planning was a very lucrative business, and I didn't have that much money to throw around. I was counting on that friends and family discount Bree had mentioned. I had a reasonable budget for the party, but I needed a discount if I wanted to put on something successful.

"It's not that easy," I said, pulling out my phone. "And she agreed to help me. She has to understand my time is just as important as hers."

"Damn," Rory said. "Laying down the law."

"Hardly. Just telling it like it is. She's not the only one with a job and a demanding schedule. She's going to have to work with me if I'm going to work with her."

I dialed her number.

"This is Pru," she answered. Then, she pulled the receiver away from her mouth and said, "No, no, not the white, the off white."

"Pru, it's Sebastian."

"You're late. I told you nine because I was at my office at nine. I am now away from my office and busy with another client. If you can't respect my time, then I can't respect yours."

This chick either had some big balls on her or she really hated me. From what little I knew about Pru, it was both.

"Okay, next time, I'll tell the mother whose infant was trapped in the backseat of her car after she was T-boned that she'll have to wait for me to get him out because my event planner's needs are more important."

Rory shoved his fist in his mouth to stifle his laugh. "We didn't even rescue an infant this morning," he whispered.

I shrugged. Pru didn't need to know that.

"I'm...I apologize. I hope everything is well."

"No fatalities, if that's what you mean, but there were a couple of hospital visits."

She cleared her throat. "When works for you?" she asked.

"I'm off at five."

"I'll see you at five."

"Five thirty," I corrected. "It'll take me a half hour to get to your office."

"Right. I will see you at five thirty."

17

I hung up the phone.

"You're a dick," Rory said, still laughing. "Making her feel guilty like that."

"Eh. She deserved it. Acting like I'd stood her up or something. I have a job, and the world doesn't revolve around her."

Rory shook his head and grinned. "I wish I could be there this afternoon when you meet with her."

"Why?"

"I just think it will be interesting, is all."

"I can guarantee it will be very boring."

———

She was late.

As soon as I had arrived, a very kind receptionist had put me in Pru's office to wait, and Pru hadn't bothered to show.

It was unbelievable that she would be so bold as to tell me I wasn't respecting her time, and here she was, not respecting mine.

I checked my watch one last time, ready to head out, when she blew through the door. She had her phone to her ear and her eyes on the large bag she was carrying.

"Listen, Kellianne, I will get on that immediately."

I cleared my throat.

Pru slowly raised her head to see me leaning against her desk with my arms crossed over my chest.

She pushed several braids behind her ear. "Kellianne, I'm going to have to call you back."

Pru held her head high as she walked around to the other side of her desk.

"You're late," I said.

She checked her phone. "Whoops, I guess I am." She sat in her chair and pulled herself up to her desk. As she folded her elegant hands and rested her elbows on the surface, she said, "Tell me what you are looking for with this event."

I narrowed my eyes. "Were you late on purpose because you hoped I would leave?"

She chuckled. "No, but that would have been nice."

"Sorry to disappoint," I said in a voice that wasn't the least bit apologetic.

Pru leaned back. "Will you please sit, so we can discuss your needs and get this over with?"

"I would tell you what my needs are, but they would probably shock you."

Her jaw dropped.

"As for the charity event, let's do it over dinner. I just finished a twelve-hour shift, and I'm starving."

Pru scoffed. "I'm not going to dinner with you."

"Honey, I'm not asking you to dinner. Don't flatter yourself. This is a work meeting *over* dinner."

Anger flared in her dark brown eyes and a hint of red hit her russet-brown cheeks as she stood and leaned forward, resting her hands on her desk. "Don't call me honey. And if I actually thought you were interested in me, I would be the furthest thing from flattered."

I mimicked her pose and got in her face. "The feeling's mutual, which is too bad."

She raised her brow in speculation. "Why?"

"Because if I was interested, I would fuck you hard enough to dislodge that stick from your ass. Maybe then you'd be in a better mood...*honey*."

Chapter Four

PRU

I POINTED my finger toward the door as Sebastian straightened. "Get out."

I could not believe he had said that to me. This was why I didn't like alpha males. They thought they could say whatever they wanted to whomever they wanted.

What I really didn't like was the way my pussy had responded to him talking about fucking me hard. I hadn't had a sexual encounter like that in so long, and unfortunately, it'd sounded all too good to the primal part of my brain.

"I'll leave as soon as you're ready to grab some food. The shit we have sitting around the firehouse is barely edible."

"We are not doing this," I said through clenched teeth.

A knock sounded at my open door, and I stepped to the side to see my boss and owner of the company.

My neck heated, and I prayed to the work gods that she

hadn't heard anything Sebastian and I had said to each other.

"Hello," my boss said, holding her hand out to Sebastian. "I'm Cherry."

Sebastian gave her a charismatic smile. "Hello, Cherry. I'm Sebastian."

My boss gave him the once-over. "Are you here for business or pleasure? I hope she's giving you her best if you are a client."

Crap.

I didn't know if Cherry had heard us arguing or if she could simply feel the tension. She had very good instincts, which was how she'd ended up running a successful business.

"I'm here as a client, but Pru is also a friend of my cousin's."

Cherry smiled. "It's always nice to get referrals. What do you need our help with?"

"A fundraiser my fire department puts on every year."

Cherry perked up like she'd heard Christmas was coming twice this year. "You aren't talking about the Annual Golden Prairie Firefighters Charity Event, are you?"

"Yes, ma'am, I am."

I gritted my teeth. He called Cherry ma'am, and I got honey.

"Pru, this is a great honor to be asked to do this," my boss said to me.

I gave her a tight smile.

Like I'd said, Cherry had good instincts, and she must have sensed my reservations.

"Sebastian, if Pru is unable to help you out with this, we have other staff who could take you on as a client."

I stiffened.

"Thank you," Sebastian said. "But since Pru was referred to me by a family member, I would really like to stay with her. If she's too busy, I will simply move on."

Cherry had to see through his whole *woe is me* attitude.

"Sebastian, would you mind stepping outside while I speak to Pru alone?"

"No problem." Sebastian went to the door and grinned at me before closing it behind him.

Cherry stepped forward and lowered her voice. "Pru, this charity event is a big deal."

"I've never even heard of it."

"Yes, you have. It's also called Fun, Fire, and Fundraising."

I had heard of it, but she had to be wrong. "Are you sure? I always thought that was the Minneapolis Fire Department."

"No, it's not."

I sat down at my desk and Googled the information. *Dammit. No.*

"You're right," I admitted.

"Of course I am."

I put my head in my hands. This was a big event that I could add to my résumé. But could I stand to work with

Sebastian on this? Should I even give him a chance when he had the audacity to talk about fucking me to my face?

The bottom line was, if he wasn't Bree's cousin, I would have said no. All our friends loved him, and it seemed Cherry did too. He had everyone else charmed, but not me, and I wasn't going to put up with the way he spoke to me.

I met my boss's eyes. "I understand how big this is and how it would look for both me and Essence Events, but I'm going to have to decline. I have two other events I'm planning right now." I added the last part, so she would think the reason I'd said no was because I was too busy.

Cherry laughed. "Oh, Pru, you misunderstand. I'm not giving you a choice. You are planning this event."

"But—"

Cherry turned her back on me. "Sebastian?"

Sebastian opened the door and peeked his head in.

"Who benefits from the charity fundraiser this year?"

"Well, half always goes to the department to help us with equipment and other needs that support the community. And the other half will go to The Children's Heart Foundation."

My boss swung back around with a smug look on her face. "Are you really going to say no to the children, Pru?"

"Yeah, Pru, are you really going to say no to the children?" Sebastian said, all innocent yet mocking at the same time.

I gritted my teeth but unclenched my jaw just enough to mutter, "No."

Cherry cupped her ear. "I'm sorry? What was that?"

"I said, no," I said louder this time. "I'll plan the fundraiser."

"I knew you would," she said. "I'll have Roberta help you out with your other events. This obviously takes precedence." She headed out my door. "Nice to meet you, Sebastian."

"You too, Cherry." When my boss was gone, he looked at me. "Are you ready to eat?"

I picked up my purse and the thick black binder I used to take notes. I liked writing stuff down versus putting everything in a computer. It helped me remember things better.

When I got to the doorway, I socked Sebastian in the gut with my purse. "You make one more comment about fucking me, and I don't care if I get fired. I'll quit."

"I won't say anything until you want me to."

I snorted. "That's never going to happen."

That should have been enough to shut him up, but he laughed and said, "We'll see about that."

Chapter Five

PRU

I CROSSED my legs and told the server, "One large glass of wine, please."

"Diet Pepsi for me," Sebastian said.

"Do you not drink?" I asked him after the server left. If he was in AA, I didn't want to be rude and have wine in front of him. Even if I wasn't a fan of his, I wasn't insensitive.

"I do. Just not tonight."

"Why?"

He leaned in. "You told me not to talk about it."

"Told you not to talk about it?"

Our server came back with our drinks. "Here you go," he said, setting them down.

"Thank you," I told him.

The man walked away, and Sebastian lifted his menu. "What are you having?"

I opened my notebook and picked up my pen. "How about we talk about what you are looking for instead?"

He looked over the top of the plastic. "But you need to eat."

Knowing he wasn't going to let it go, I quickly picked something. "A quesadilla."

"Sounds good. I think I'm going to have steak."

"Now, can we talk about what you are looking for?"

Sebastian closed his menu and sighed, as if we weren't both here because of him. I didn't even want to be planning this thing.

"I need a large space, obviously, where we can have dinner. I've been told they've used the convention center a lot in the past, but I'm open to other ideas."

I immediately had several spots in mind. "How much per plate?"

"Enough to raise some money, but not enough that you have to be uber rich to attend."

"That's very nice of you, but the richer people are, the more money they're likely to spend once attending the event."

He laughed. "Says who?"

"Me."

"Do you even know any rich people?"

I flicked my pen back and forth. "I've worked with numerous wealthy people in my time."

"And they're stingy."

At events, I had seen people drop thousands of dollars on silly items. "No, they're not—" I cut myself off when I remembered one of those same couples who wouldn't pay for their teenage kid's Uber because they could walk the three miles home. In the winter.

"Ah, you agree with me." Sebastian smiled.

"I never said that, but I've got it. *Plates not too expensive*," I said and wrote it down. "What else are you thinking to raise money?"

"I have a list of companies who donate items every year for people to bid on."

"So, a silent auction?"

"Yes."

"Do you have that list?" I asked, expecting him to pull it out of his pocket or something.

"Yes."

I raised my brow. "Do you think you can get it to me?"

"I'll email it."

"Sooner rather than later, please."

He picked up his phone.

"You don't have to do it—never mind." There was no point in wasting my breath.

A minute later, he set his phone down. "Done."

"I'll look over the list later and let you know if we should add more. You might have to ask around for donations."

He grinned. "I can do that."

"I'm sure you can," I muttered.

I was sure that he could get plenty of things from others if he asked.

"Is there a theme to this event?"

Sebastian stared blankly at me.

"I take it, that's a no."

"Can we do something with the foundation we're donating to? Something with hearts?"

"That's a good idea, but hearts might make people think romance." I rapped my pen against my notebook. "I'll have to think on this." I jotted down a few notes. "I'm guessing I have free rein for the theme?"

"Hmm?"

I looked up to see Sebastian almost in a daze.

"Do I have the authority to give the event a theme?"

"Oh, sure."

I wrote down *hearts, not romantic* as a reminder to come back to it later. "Okay, so we're working on theme. We have dinner and a silent auction. Anything else to raise money?"

"No."

"Are we going to do a bachelor auction?"

"A what now?"

I blinked at him. "You don't know what a bachelor auction is?"

He shrugged. "No."

"It's where we auction off dates with the single guys you work with."

"I work with women too."

"That's fine. We can do a bachelor-slash-bachelorette auction."

He frowned. "Why?"

"Because you're firefighters. Jeez, Sebastian, you can't

tell me you've never had women interested in you just because of your job and uniform."

He chuckled. "Of course I have. They're called bunker bunnies, badge bunnies, uniform chasers, hose hos, hose honeys, fireflies, fire hos, hero chasers, turnout chasers, hose lovers, fire bunnies—"

Holding up my hand, I cut him off. "I get it. But you are proving my point. If you and your coworkers auctioned yourselves off, you could bring in a lot of money."

His eyes went wide. "You mean, like, for fucking?"

"No, not for...sex."

Sebastian snickered.

"But you already knew that." *Asshole.*

He lifted his glass to his lips and smiled. "Maybe I did. Maybe I didn't," he said and took a sip.

I chose to ignore his teasing. "We can call that part of the night A Date with a Firefighter." I tapped my chin. "Or maybe we should do Dinner with a Firefighter." I made a few more notes.

Our server returned at that point to take our food order, which gave me a few moments to think.

After we were alone again, I asked, "This charity event is a big deal. Why are they having a firefighter plan it? Your department must have administrative people who manage stuff like this?"

"Someone has to approve all this, but it's always planned by firefighters because that's the fun of it. Usually, it's two or three, but my captain doesn't care for me, so he gave only me the project."

That was something his captain and I had in common. I wondered what Sebastian had done to piss the man off.

"Brutal. But what did you do?"

Sebastian's face grew serious, and his mouth turned down. "I didn't do anything. He doesn't like that a guy from out of state came in and got the ranking of lieutenant. He'd wanted it to go to someone else, but I had more experience. It also helped that I'd trained and started out working in Minnesota, but he's holding a grudge."

"I apologize. I was joking about the *what did you do* thing."

"No, you weren't, but that's okay."

I looked down and fiddled with the stem of my wineglass. "No, it's not." But I didn't want to talk about this any longer. "I was thinking, what if you did something where people could bring their kids to the fire station to tour? You could sell, like, ten tickets or something."

"We already do those for free if people ask."

"What about riding around for a day?"

He slowly shook his head. "I don't think they would go for that."

"I understand. I'll keep brainstorming."

"I think the dinner and the silent auction are going to be good enough."

I straightened my back. "What about the bachelor-bachelorette auction?"

"I don't want to do that. And I doubt my fellow firefighters would either."

Bringing in a lot of money for this year's fundraiser

would look very good for me. There had to be some way I could convince him.

"You don't know until you ask. You shouldn't assume," I said. "And I was thinking, is your captain single?"

"He is."

"What would your captain think about doing the dinner or date with a firefighter?"

"Oh, I know he'd hate it."

"Then, I think that's a really good reason for you to say yes."

Sebastian waited a beat. "I'll think about it."

Chapter Six

SEBASTIAN

I HELD the door open for Pru and followed her outside the restaurant.

"Oh man."

"What's wrong?" I asked, following her line of sight.

She pointed. "There's a new bar over there that just opened."

"Pour Choices?"

"Yes. I thought that wasn't opening until next week. I completely missed it in the daylight. If I had known, I would have had us go and eat there."

"I like the name." It gave me a chuckle. "Is it important that you go there?"

"I always check out things right away. You never know when someone might be looking for a hip, new place. Or maybe they want a particular vibe. It's my job to find the perfect places for everything—from small gatherings to big events, like yours."

I shrugged. "Let's go over there then," I said, ready to cross the street.

Pru laughed. "We can't go now."

"Why?"

"I have to work in the morning, and I assume you do too."

"Not till five. And it's only"—I checked my watch—"a little after seven right now. We have time."

Pru looked at me and then back at the bar. With a sigh, she said, "Why not?"

When we walked in, I was surprised to see how many people were here on a Thursday evening. It was bigger on the inside than it appeared on the outside.

"Looks like people like it," I said, leaning close to Pru so she could hear me.

"Yeah, that's a good sign."

Her breath tickled my neck, and I had to suddenly shove my dick around in my pants. If she saw I had a hard-on, she'd leave the bar in a heartbeat.

"Where should we sit? Table, booth, or bar?"

"Bar. I like to get a feel for how the staff works."

I pulled out a stool for her and took a seat at the one next to her.

"Are you always a gentleman, or are you trying to get on my nice side?" she asked.

I shook my head. "I don't know what you mean. I'm the guy you got mad at for saying something about fucking you."

She rolled her eyes and faced the bartender coming our way. "Can I get a drink, please?"

The bartender grinned. "Sure. What do you want?"

Pru tilted her head and smiled. "How about you come up with something for me?"

"Will do." He turned to me. "And for you, sir?"

"I'll have a beer."

"Coming right up."

Pru looked at me. "I thought you weren't drinking?"

I lifted a shoulder. "That was at dinner." And that had been before Pru had three glasses of wine. "And it's only a beer. It's not going to get me drunk." I moved close until I could smell her perfume. "Unlike whatever it is you're having." I nodded toward the big glass with a yellow-and-orange drink that the bartender placed in front of her. "You are going to be shit-faced after that."

"I'll be fine," she said as she turned her head in my direction.

Our lips were inches away, but I sat back. I didn't mess with women who were intoxicated, especially when I wasn't.

"I guess we'll see."

Pru wrapped her lips around her straw and sucked. She sat back a few seconds later. "Whew. That's strong."

I snorted. "Told you."

Pushing her glass my way, she asked, "Want to try?"

"No." I didn't care for fruity drinks.

"Pussy," she teased.

I shrugged. "You are what you eat."

Her mouth dropped open, and I pushed her chin back up.

"Don't be so shocked. Most men eat pussy," I told her.

She scoffed. "But they don't talk about it."

I took a sip of my beer. "They should. Pussy is delicious, and you get to make a woman come. Win-win, in my opinion."

Pru shifted on her stool.

"You okay?"

"Yeah." She sucked half her drink down. "But I think I need to use the restroom. I'll be back. Watch my drink, will you?"

"Consider it done."

After Pru left, I picked up my phone to kill some time. Someone lowered the lights as eight p.m. hit, and while I was aware that more people had come into the bar, I didn't pay them much mind.

Pru came back a few minutes later, but I was in the middle of reading an email from my mother about some family stuff happening, and I wanted to finish it, so I wouldn't forget to go back to it later.

"Hello, beautiful," I heard a deep voice say.

I peeked my head up to see a guy standing on the other side of Pru.

"Hey," she said, her voice flat and clearly uninviting.

I didn't blame her. The dude had slicked-back hair, a nice suit, and a watch that cost more than I made in a year. His whole persona screamed money. But his arrogance was even louder. This guy had no problem getting women, and he knew it.

Pru just wasn't going to be one of them.

Slick got down on his forearms to get closer to her. "What do you say? You want to get out of here?"

"No."

Slick laughed. "Playing hard to get, are we?"

I gritted my teeth. What was wrong with men, thinking every woman wanted them?

This whole thing was embarrassing.

But I kept my head down. Pru would let me know if she needed me to jump in.

"How about I buy you another drink?"

Pru pushed her empty glass to the edge of the bar and spun around on her stool. "No. N-O. I don't want a drink from you. I don't want to leave the bar with you. I don't want anything to do with you. I am not playing hard to get. I'm honestly telling you to go away."

I stifled a laugh with a cough as Pru twisted her stool around to me.

"Can you believe this guy?" she hissed at me.

"Unfortunately, yes," I had to admit. There were a lot of assholes out there.

Slick stood back up. "This your woman?" he asked me. "She needs to be taught some manners."

I put my phone down and sighed. This guy didn't know when to quit, and since he'd addressed me, I supposed it was my turn to step in. "No, she is not my woman. She is her own woman. And, no, she doesn't need to be taught some manners." Pointing my finger at him, I said, "You do. She told you she wasn't interested, but you can't get that through your Neanderthal brain." I cupped my mouth with my hands. "She doesn't want you."

"Whatever." He scoffed and got in Pru's face. "I don't want a bitch like you anyway."

I winced, knowing he'd messed with the wrong person.

Pru snatched his junk and squeezed.

Slick went up on his tippy-toes and whined like a dog.

"Listen to me. I am not a bitch just because I don't want your attention. I was polite until you pushed me. I do not owe you anything. *Women* don't owe you anything. No means no. Got it?"

Slick nodded, and Pru released him.

He looked like he wanted to punch her, so I slid off my stool. I was six-two and well over two hundred pounds. I was taller and had more muscle, and I wanted him to know I wasn't going to let him hurt her. Although Pru would probably win if they got in a physical altercation anyway.

"Is there a problem over here?" one of the bartenders came over and asked.

Slick held up his hands. "Nope. I was just leaving."

"Can I get either of you anything?" the bartender asked after Slick walked away.

"No," I said at the same time Pru told him, "I'll have another of whatever this is."

I shook my head at the guy, and to Pru, I said, "I think it's time for us to call it a night. We both have to work tomorrow."

She sighed but agreed. "You're probably right." She moved to get off her stool, but she got her foot caught in the side and fell into me.

She started laughing, and I realized that she was no longer sober.

Picking her up under her arms, I set her upright. "Come on. I'll give you a ride home."

When we got to the door, she stopped me. "Thanks for not muscling your way in back there."

"You're welcome." It seemed like an odd thing to be thankful for.

She grinned and swayed toward me until our chests touched. "When I grabbed his crotch, did it make your dick and balls shrivel up in fear?"

I snickered. "I hate to disappoint you, but no. It made me hard."

She gasped. "No way. I don't believe you." And before I could stop her, her hand slid down the front of my pants and grasped my very stiff cock. "Oh my God, you're not lying. Why are you hard?"

I scoffed at the obvious question. "Because it was hot, watching you tell him off. Now, would you mind removing your hand, so we can get you home?"

"How about you come to my place and use this"—she squeezed my shaft—"on me instead?"

I wrapped my fingers around her wrist and gently tugged. "I don't have sex with drunk chicks."

"Don't you mean, fuck?"

She emphasized the *F* sound, drawing her lip from under her teeth, and my dick jumped in her fist.

I leaned forward and put my mouth next to her ear. "As much as I want to rub it in your face that you want me to fuck you when earlier tonight, you said that was never going to happen, I can't. It wouldn't be right." I kissed her below the ear and yanked hard enough that she let me go.

She looked up at me with hooded eyes and repeated my words back to me. "We'll see about that."

Chapter Seven

PRU

"PRU."

I groaned.

"Pru. Open your eyes."

Squinting, I did just that.

My head hurt, and it took me a second to assess my surroundings.

I was in a bed that was not my own. The room was dark, except for the bright hall light that shone in, and Sebastian was sitting on the edge of the mattress.

"Oh my God, we didn't have sex, did we?" I whined.

He chuckled but responded with a simple, "No."

"What's so funny about that?" I asked as the memory of grabbing his dick and asking him to fuck me came back to me. I hadn't been *that* intoxicated, but drunk Pru was also horny Pru, and whether or not I wanted to admit it, I was attracted to Sebastian. "Never mind," I quickly added before he could answer.

I slowly sat up and winced. I wasn't exactly hungover, but I did have a headache. I wasn't as young as I used to be.

"Here." Sebastian handed me a glass of water and a couple pills. "This will help you feel better."

"Thank you," I said, taking both from him. I swallowed the medicine and drank half the glass.

"It's only about a quarter after four, but you are welcome to stay and sleep off some of your headache."

I fell back on the bed. "Why are you up so early?"

"I have to get to work. And I had one beer last night. Although sleeping on the couch wasn't the most comfortable, I still got a solid six hours."

I froze. "You slept on the couch? Wait. Am I in your bed?"

He chuckled. "Yeah. Where did you think you were?"

"The guest room."

"I have one of those. I just don't have a bed in it."

I pulled the covers over my nose to hide until I realized the sheets smelled like him. I shoved them back down and kicked them off.

"I should go. I did not mean to take your bed. I'm sorry about that." I should apologize for touching his cock, too, but that wasn't going to happen. I swung my legs to the floor as a thought occurred to me. I narrowed my eyes at him. "Why did you bring me here? Why didn't you take me home? Are you sure we didn't have sex?"

I knew I was being a bitch because I had all my clothes on from last night, down to my uncomfortable bra. I remembered everything from the night before by now, and

I was totally the one who had hit on him. If we had ended up sleeping together, it would have all been on me. However, my pride wouldn't admit it out loud. In fact, my ego had taken a hit.

I had muttered, "We'll see about that," to him with all the confidence of a drunk woman.

Yeah, *we hadn't seen about that.* He'd turned me down, and I'd looked like a jerk.

"Don't flatter yourself." Sebastian stood. "You fell asleep in the car, and I couldn't wake you up, so I brought you here. Did you know that you snore?"

I gasped. "I've been working long hours lately. I must have been super tired."

He held up his hands and laughed. "Whatever you say."

He shifted his hips to face the direction of the doorway, and suddenly, it was like a spotlight was on his body. He had on a slim-fitted T-shirt that was so thin that I could see the outline of his muscles. And don't get me started on his track pants. Everyone always talked about gray sweatpants. *Gray sweatpants this, gray sweatpants that.* Had any of these women looked at a man in thin nylon pants? Because, damn, he looked good.

And now, I was recalling exactly the way he'd felt in my hand last night. Of course Sebastian had a big dick. And with his confidence, I had no doubt that he knew how to use it too.

I wondered what he would feel like inside me. Would he go slow and make sure he hit all the right spots, or would he fuck me so hard that I'd ache the next day?

Nope, nope, nope. I needed to get my mind back on track and off Sebastian. He was nothing but my friend's cousin and my new client.

I jumped up, and he backed up.

He cocked an eyebrow. "You okay?"

I supposed I looked like I was freaking out when all we had been talking about was me falling asleep in his car.

"Yes. I just need to get home and get to work. I have a fiftieth birthday party happening tonight, and I need to make sure everything is ready."

"No rest for the wicked," he said in a low voice.

"That's right. You remember that," I warned.

"Ooh," he said, waving his hands in mock fear. He turned on his heel and headed for the door. "Let's go. If we leave now, I can give you a quick ride to the restaurant to get your car."

Before he got to the door, Sebastian shoved his hands in his pockets, pulling his pants over his ass.

Dammit. He had a nice butt too.

But this fine specimen of a man reminded me of our conversation at dinner last night.

Rushing after him, I said, "Hey, have you thought more about the Date with a Firefighter auction?"

He stopped and did a half-turn. "You're not going to let this go, are you?"

I laughed. "No. You could bring in so much money with this."

He took a hand out of his pocket and stroked his beard. "I'll tell you what."

My ears perked. This sounded hopeful. "What?"

"If you do it, I'll do it."

I wrinkled my nose. "The auction? I can't. I'm not a firefighter, and I'm planning the event. I will be working the whole night."

"Not that auction, just *an* auction."

No way. "You want me to find an auction and just sign myself up? I could end up on a date with a rapist or a serial killer." I shuddered. "Or someone who hasn't showered in a week." I gagged on my tongue.

Sebastian grinned and waved a finger at me. "Ahh, she gets it now. We don't want to be pimped out by you for money." He continued on to his front door.

I grabbed his arm. "Wait."

He kept walking, dragging me with him. "What?" he said when we got to the entryway.

"The fundraiser will be different. It will be full of classy people. And it's just dinner. In a public place," I quickly added. "And you haven't even asked anyone yet. You're answering no for everyone."

"So, find another classy auction and get yourself on that list. *It's just dinner.* Right, Pru?"

I chewed on my lip. "Okay, I will find a place."

A smile spread across his face. "I need to be there to see. I'm there, or it didn't happen."

I hadn't even considered faking it. I needed more sleep because that would have been a good idea. "Deal."

Sebastian rubbed his hands together. "I can't wait."

———

When I got home, I showered before lying down for another hour or so. As much work as I needed to do that day, I knew I would do better with more shut-eye than without.

But after I woke up again, I realized what I had said yes to with Sebastian. I had no idea where I was going to find some sort of date or dinner auction. Especially one with female participants. It was more common to have an auction with bachelors than bachelorettes.

Once at work, I sent out an email to all my coworkers to see if they were planning any events with an auction, but by noon, I had turned up empty.

I sat back in my chair and closed my eyes.

"What are you doing?"

I sat up to see my coworker and friend Billie walk into my office.

"Stressful day?"

"Yes, and no," I answered. "You?"

"I have tonight off, but tomorrow will be busy." She sat down in the chair across from me. "What's wrong?"

I laughed because my problem seemed so silly, just thinking about saying it out loud.

"Okay, now, you have to tell me," Billie said.

I quickly explained the deal Sebastian and I had made.

"Am I making a mistake?" I asked.

Billie shook her head. "Not at all. A date with a fireman? A man in uniform? Even if they're not good-looking, this is going to raise money."

I sighed and picked at the corner of my desk. "But how am I going to find something for myself?"

"Pru, you are an event planner. Plan an event. You can think of something." Billie looked down at her phone in her hand. "I have to go. I just wanted to stop by and say hi."

Waving to her as she walked out, I thought about what she'd said.

I *was* an event planner. There had to be something I could do.

I tapped my fingers against my armrest for a few minutes until, suddenly, it was there.

The perfect idea had come to me.

Chapter Eight

SEBASTIAN

"SEBASTIAN, SOMEONE'S HERE FOR YOU."

I took my last bite of lunch as one of my coworkers showed Pru into the kitchen.

"What are you doing here?" I asked as she came over and sat adjacent to me. Across from her was an empty chair that I'd pulled up to rest my feet on.

"I came to talk to you about a few things," she said, opening her binder and pulling out a stack of papers.

"You've been busy." I was surprised, as it was only Tuesday.

We'd exchanged a few texts and emails since we'd left my house on Friday, but this was the first time we'd spoken.

She handed me a piece of paper. "I know that the charity event has been held at the same venue for the last five years, but a year ago, the convention center almost doubled their prices, and they've upped them again this year."

"Oof. That's not good." I looked over the sheet that listed the prices and amenities. "Do we have other options?"

"That's my question to you. Can we hold it somewhere else, or do we have to use this location?"

"I haven't been told anything about needing to use this place."

Pru beamed. "I was hoping you'd say that." She pulled her phone out of her pocket. "This is an old warehouse that someone bought recently and fixed up. Look at the pictures," she said, handing me her cell.

I started scrolling as she kept talking.

"I thought it would be perfect with it being a fire department charity event."

She was right. The exposed brick and the high ceilings would look nice.

"It won't be as fancy." I had seen pictures of previous events.

"But that's okay. You don't want the plates to be outrageously expensive. The atmosphere will be relaxing." Out came another sheet of paper with a diagram of the layout. "Here is where the stage will be. Then all the tables. And we can put the items for the silent auction back in this area."

"Is there a catch?"

She chuckled. "Kind of. The convention center has their own kitchen and catering staff, so we will have to hire outside. That can be a good thing or a bad thing, depending on how you feel."

"I think it's a good thing," a voice said.

We looked up to see Rory standing there.

"Last year, the chicken was dry, and the year before, my steak was overcooked. I, for one, welcome something new."

"Pru, this is Rory. Rory, this is Pru, the event planner."

Pru held out her hand, and Rory kissed the back of it.

"Nice to meet you."

"Likewise."

"Although we kind of already met."

Pru frowned.

"I was there the night you handed Sebastian your card."

"Oh. Sorry about not saying hi. I was in a hurry."

Yeah. A hurry to get away from me.

"No big deal. I get it." He looked at all the papers lying on the table. "So, what are the food options? Please tell me you have some good ones."

"I do..." Pru got a look in her eye that I didn't trust. "But I have a question for you first."

"For me?" Rory asked. "Shoot. Go ahead and ask."

"Are you single?"

I groaned as Rory's eyes flicked to mine.

"She's not asking you out, dude. She wants to know how you feel about a bachelor auction."

"You mean, like one of those things where you'd bring me onstage and auction me off to every pretty lady in the audience? Heck yeah. Count me in."

"Not all of them will be pretty," I said, trying to get him on my side.

Rory put his hand on my shoulder and shook his head. "Sebastian, they're all pretty."

I knocked it away. "You're not helping."

"Oh, he most certainly is helping," Pru said. She leaned forward. "What do you think the others will say to my idea?" She put her hand up. "And I should preface that it's not really a bachelor auction. It will be an auction for a dinner with a firefighter. All the firefighters can participate. And dinner sounds like less pressure than a date."

Rory frowned, and I could tell he was confused. He was probably thinking dinner was a date.

"Dinner is less formal, and there's no expectation of putting out," I explained.

Rory laughed. "Good one."

I raised my brow.

"Oh, you're serious."

Pru looked at him in disbelief. "Yes, he's serious. Sex absolutely cannot be a part of the auction. It's for fun and to raise money."

"Aw shucks. And here I thought, I was going to get some."

I looked away and shook my head.

"Don't shake your head at me," Rory said, pointing a finger my way.

"I wasn't."

"We can't all get laid as much as you."

I discreetly nodded my head toward Pru. "Not in front of the guest," I said in a low voice.

"I'm fine," Pru said, patting my arm. "I was under no illusions that Sebastian was a virgin."

Slicing my hand through the air, I said, "Can we not talk about my sex life, please?"

"Gladly." Pru looked at Rory. "Do you think your other single coworkers would agree with doing this dinner auction too?"

"I think so. Anything to raise money. But I'll go ask around and send some texts."

Pru smiled at him like she had to the bartender the other night and lifted her shoulders up to make herself seem sweet and innocent. "Thank you, Rory."

As soon as Rory left, I looked at her. "If you think asking everyone else and getting them to say yes will make me change my mind, you are wrong. We had a deal, and I'm still in charge of this thing."

"Oh, I know." She gave me a smug smile. "Are you free on Saturday night? Not this weekend, but the next."

My eyebrows rose. "Are you asking me out?"

"No."

"Then, yes."

She scowled, as if she hadn't just immediately rejected me first with her abrupt no.

"What's going on?" I asked.

The corner of her mouth tilted up. "I am going to be in an auction. Just as you requested."

I dropped my feet to the floor and twisted my body toward her. "*Bullshit.*"

"Bull-true."

I had been counting on Pru not finding another auction, and here, she had done it in less than a week.

"Where?" I asked, still not quite believing her.

"A friend from college is having a bachelorette party next weekend. I unofficially said I would help her, especially since her party is at her parents' bar. Her mom was in a car accident about six months ago and still hasn't fully recovered, and they have a lot of debt. My friend and her soon-to-be husband also haven't been able to afford a honeymoon because of this. She helps out at the bar with her mom not able to work, and her fiancé is overseas in the military, so neither of them can get a second job."

I could already guess the rest of this story.

"I called her and asked if her bridesmaids would be interested in doing an auction to help her and her family raise money. Half will go to her mom's medical bills, and the other will go to her honeymoon." Pru shrugged. "All her bridesmaids said yes, and she even has some other single friends who have volunteered, including me."

"You think you're so smart, don't you?"

She moved to the edge of her seat and got nose to nose with me. "I don't think anything. I *am* smart, Sebastian. And if you're not careful, I'm going to get the best of you."

I put my hand around her waist and yanked her closer. Putting my mouth against her ear, I said, "Not if I get you first."

Even though I had turned Pru down last Thursday, I knew one thing for sure.

I was fucking this woman. No ifs, ands, or buts. She was going to be under me—and soon.

Because nothing was hotter than her big fucking brain.

Chapter Nine

PRU

SEBASTIAN RAN his nose down the inside of my neck as I slowly tilted my head to the side.

"Is everything okay here?"

I snapped back from Sebastian and pushed my chair away.

I put a smile on my face for Rory and told him, "Yep." But inside, I was overheated and flustered. My pussy was on fire with want. "Sebastian and I are just finishing up."

He frowned and rested his hands on his flat stomach. "We are? We haven't even discussed catering."

I started shoving the information I had brought back into my binder. "I can text you. Or call you. Or email you." That was for the best. The least personal.

"Well, I just came back to let you know that everyone who is here today is up for the dinner auction."

My shoulders sagged as I looked up at Rory. "Thank

you so much for asking. Would you mind finding out what the others think?"

He smiled. "It would be my pleasure. I'll send an email now."

"Thank you."

Rory took off, and I was alone with Sebastian again.

He put his hand on top of mine. "You don't have to leave. I don't bite."

I jerked my appendage out from under his and zipped up my binder. "Is that where you add, *hard*?"

Sebastian frowned in confusion and then busted out laughing. "*I don't bite—hard*," he repeated and shook his head. "Why do you think everything I say is sexual in nature?" His eyes scanned me up and down. "Are you hard up or something?"

I straightened my spine because I was more hard up than he knew. "It's because I've been around men like you my whole life, and most of them use a lot of sexual innuendos."

His arms went across his chest as I felt his defenses rise. "And what kind of man am I?"

I stood to give us more space and to make me feel like I had some semblance of control. "I really hate to use the term because so many guys use it wrong, but you're an alpha male."

Sebastian laughed again and dropped his arms. "What the fuck? You're telling me I'm one of those assholes who spouts a bunch of bullshit on social media about being an alpha male?"

I sighed. This was why I hadn't wanted to say anything.

"No, you're not. That's why I said so many men use it wrong. Real alpha males don't actually have to tell anyone they're alpha; they just are. And many people say that all that alpha/beta stuff doesn't actually exist, but I think it does on some level." I lifted my chin. "And you are an alpha male."

"Okay, I'll play. What does it mean then?"

I didn't want to talk about this, and I regretted bringing it up. "You're confident and good-looking, but a big part of your appeal is your confidence."

"So, you're saying, I could be ugly and still attractive because I'm confident?"

"Basically. Look at..." I struggled to come up with a good example for him. "Jon Bernthal."

"Who?"

"He was on Netflix's *The Punisher*. My ex thought he was so unattractive and that if I met him on the street, I probably wouldn't be that impressed either. But in *The Punisher*?" I fanned my face. "He was so hot. Frank Castle is an alpha male and super sexy."

"Who's Frank Castle?"

"Forget this. I'm done."

I shifted to step away, but Sebastian put his hand on my wrist.

"I'm kidding. I know Frank Castle is The Punisher. But is that all? You think I'm sexy?"

I groaned as he grinned.

"I said Jon Bernthal is sexy. I never said *you* were sexy."

He licked his lips. "You didn't have to."

I pointed a finger at him. "See? That right there. That's what I'm talking about."

He held his hands up at his sides. "I'm only giving you crap."

I put a hand on the table and leaned over. "Okay, hypothetical question."

"Okay."

"What if I told you that I did find you sexy versus if I didn't?"

His eyes moved down my body, almost as if he were caressing it. When he got back to my face, he asked, "You want the whole truth or the PG version?"

I knew I was going to regret it, but I told him, "The whole truth."

"I'd slide my hand up that skirt of yours to see if you were as wet as I hoped you were. Then, I'd push my fingers inside you, stroking you until you came. I'd send you home after that with the promise that I'd be over later to fuck you."

I had to catch my breath. "Would you make sure I came again when we had sex?"

He jerked his head back and scowled. "Of course I would. I'd make sure you came multiple times, but more importantly, I'd make sure you came on my cock." He lowered his lids. "But what does that have to do with me being an alpha male?"

It didn't have anything to do with it. "Okay, so now, what would you do if I felt the opposite?"

He shrugged and put his hands behind his head. "Nothing. You don't want me? It's not a big deal. There will be someone else out there who does."

How he could go from talking dirty to me to being so nonchalant, I would never understand because my underwear was soaked.

"That's what I thought," I said, straightening.

"And what does that prove?" He was clearly mystified.

"That you're more confident than most men. Would Rory say the same thing as you? We both know he wouldn't. If he knew a woman liked him, he'd be too excited to hide his feelings. And if he was interested in someone and they didn't like him back, he'd be crushed. You just go with whatever comes your way."

"Okay, but I still don't understand what the problem is."

"The problem is, you probably don't hear no a lot because people do what you want them to. And I'm not talking about sex. When you moved here, did you have to fight for your position? You came from out of state, but there were probably internal applicants who were just as qualified—or at least applicants from Minnesota."

"So, I know my worth. What's wrong with that? Too many people don't."

"True. But sometimes, that worth can be inflated because of all that confidence. So, even though you might think you deserve something, you don't."

Sebastian did not look impressed.

"And when I say *you*, I mean, people in general." I didn't want him to be offended, which, to me, just proved that he was an alpha male. I should just leave and let him be pissed off. But I had one more thing to add.

"The other problem is, while that *take it or leave it* attitude can be hot from the outside, if you're in a relationship with an alpha, it can be hard. You feel like you're the only one invested sometimes because they know they can leave and find someone else. And forget compromise. Alpha males do what they want, and they don't care if their partner is happy. And the worst part is, they don't even notice any of that."

"You sound like you're speaking from experience," Sebastian said in a low voice.

He was right. I was. Confident men turned me on, but it was hard to be with one for all the reasons I'd listed. But I didn't want him to feel sorry for me because I sure didn't.

"Eh," I said, letting him know my past relationships weren't a big deal. "It ultimately comes down to, I don't like being bossed around, and alpha males love to be in charge." I bumped my fists together. "We always end up bumping heads."

He seemed to pick up on the fact that I didn't want any pity because he smiled.

"So, let me get this straight. You think I'm confident, bossy, good-looking, don't like to hear the word *no*, and bad at relationships?"

"Not all relationships. You just don't like being with other strong people."

He slowly nodded his head. "Okay, but you forgot one thing."

"What's that?"

"I'm fucking fantastic in bed."

I shoved his head to the side as I turned to walk away. "Ugh. I'm outta here."

But I had no doubt in my mind that what he'd said was the truth.

Chapter Ten

PRU

THE NIGHT of the bachelorette auction, I was feeling nervous. There were so many uncertainties. My thoughts ranged from *what if no one bids on me* to *what if some creep bids on me.* I didn't know which was worse.

Obviously, I didn't want to have to go on a date with someone who I wasn't comfortable with, but—and I hated to admit this—I was going to be very embarrassed if no one wanted to go on a date with me. Marissa, my friend from college who was getting married, had some gorgeous friends.

Sebastian had insisted on the two of us going together, telling me he wasn't going to let me chicken out and not show up or leave early. I'd told him that wouldn't happen, but I wasn't so sure.

He lived closer to the bar, so I went to his house. When he answered the door, I'd almost forgotten how attractive he was.

I hadn't seen him in over a week. Not since I'd left the firehouse. All our communication had been done through phone and email. The good thing was, besides everyone agreeing to participate in the firefighter auction, Sebastian was actually easy to work with.

"Damn," he said. "Are you planning to bring home all the money tonight?"

I looked down at my outfit. I had on a semi-revealing black top. It dipped low and showed off the girls rather nicely. I'd paired it with dark blue jeans that shaped my ass beautifully and black high heels. I wasn't dressed that sexy.

I put a hand on my hip. "I thought I looked good."

"You look fucking gorgeous. That's the problem."

I frowned. "Problem?"

"Never mind. Let's go." He stepped back from the door and held it open for me to enter.

"What are you doing? Aren't you coming out?"

"I'm driving. We're going to go through the garage."

"Why are you driving?"

"Because I want to."

I huffed and entered his house. "This is what I meant by alpha male."

Sebastian laughed. "Thank you."

"That was not a compliment."

———

When we got to Marissa's parents' bar, Manny's Tavern, she ran up to me and wrapped her arms around me.

"Thank you for coming." Marissa stepped back and smiled at Sebastian. "And you, sir, must be the person to thank for this ingenious idea. My fiancé and I have been feeling guilty about even having a wedding, but my mom insisted. And now, we might get to have a small honeymoon."

Sebastian smiled and then quickly looked away. Could it be that he was embarrassed? Maybe he wasn't as alpha as I'd thought he was.

"I would like to take credit, but Pru really came up with this whole thing."

"Then, I thank you both." Marissa waved her hand toward the room. "Come in and meet everyone, Sebastian."

Marissa introduced Sebastian to her father first. "This is my dad, Manny. Proprietor and head bartender."

"Nice to meet you." Sebastian shook his hand.

"Same here. What can I get you?"

"Beer, please."

"Pru, what would you like?"

"I'll have a beer too."

"Coming right up."

As soon as Manny stepped away, Marissa said, "Uh-oh."

"What's *uh-oh*?" Sebastian asked.

"When Pru drinks beer, it means she wants to get some."

"Not true," I protested.

"In my experience, it doesn't happen with just beer," Sebastian said dryly.

Marissa's eyes widened. "Oh." Her eyes shot back and forth between us. "Are you two—"

"*No*," we both said.

She looked away. "Well, maybe you should."

Manny brought back our drinks just as some women ran up to us.

"Pru, Sebastian, these are my bridesmaids and friends, Dawn and Callie. They're going to be part of the auction."

Dawn put her hand up to partly block her mouth and asked Marissa, "Is Sebastian single?" But it was still loud enough that we all heard.

Marissa chuckled. "I think so."

"Yes, I am," Sebastian answered with a smile.

Dawn slid up to him and put her arm through his. "I'm single, too, so if you feel like bidding on someone, I'm your lady."

Sebastian took a sip of his beer, his neck arching and his throat moving as he did so. "Good to know," he replied, making eye contact with Dawn, to the point that she blushed.

He was being flirty with her.

"Sebastian isn't bidding on anyone tonight. He's here to observe," I snapped in a firm voice.

He smirked at me as Dawn said, "That's too bad."

Yeah, too bad.

"Pru." Someone nudged my arm. "Pru."

I tore my eyes away from Sebastian and Dawn and looked at Marissa. I had to unclench my jaw to talk. "Yeah?"

"Callie asked you a question."

"I'm sorry. What was the question?"

"Do you have anyone here to bid on you tonight?"

"No." I hated to admit that after watching Dawn drool over Sebastian. "But maybe I'll get lucky, and some handsome man will sweep me off my feet."

Callie smiled. "I don't have anyone either. Maybe you and I can stick together."

"Works for me," I said, forcing cheer into my voice. For some reason, I wasn't as excited as I had been when I first arrived.

"Pru."

I looked in the direction of where my name was being called and saw Elizabeth and Isabelle had shown up. My mood improved upon seeing my two friends.

"You both came," I said, giving them hugs. I stepped back. "Marissa, it's been a while, but do you remember Isabelle and Elizabeth?"

Marissa smiled. "I do."

"I know it's not customary to invite outside friends to a bachelorette party, but they're single, and they wanted to help out."

Marissa held her arms out. "The more, the merrier. Welcome to the party."

We all chuckled, and Marissa introduced my friends to her friends.

"How is this going to work?" Elizabeth asked.

"My dad"—Marissa turned around and pointed to her dad, who waved—"is going to be the MC. He'll make an announcement about each of you before inviting you onstage. And then we'll let the bidding begin."

"What are the rules?" Isabelle asked.

"The audience will be bidding for a date. But the candidate gets to pick the date activity, not the bidder. So, you don't have to do anything you don't want. You can choose to go to a restaurant during the day or"—she wiggled her eyebrows—"you can have a candlelit dinner at home. You pick."

"Yeah, if a super-old guy bids on me, we aren't doing anything romantic," Callie said.

"Same," I muttered.

Dawn looked up at Sebastian. "If a sexy guy bids on me, I'm going to make the date be in my bedroom."

Normally, I would agree that a woman could do whatever she wanted. I hated slut-shaming. But the thought of her and Sebastian having sex really got under my skin. I didn't want that image near my brain.

"Marissa," Manny said. "Here are the notecards."

"Thanks, Dad."

Marissa handed each of us a notecard and a pen. "Write what you want my dad to say to introduce you."

Everyone split up to find a seat in order to have a flat surface to write out their intro. Since Sebastian and I were already at the bar, I just turned around. I was surprised to see Sebastian turning around too.

I looked around him to see Dawn had found a table.

"Aren't you going to go and sit with your new friend?"

"Nope." Sebastian lifted his bottle to his lips and took another sip while keeping eye contact with me.

"Do you want to bid on her?"

"You told me I couldn't," he said instead of answering my question.

"Do you want to?"

"No."

Chapter Eleven

SEBASTIAN

BEFORE PRU COULD QUESTION why I didn't want to bid on Dawn, I asked her, "What are you putting down for your introduction?"

"What do you think I should put?"

I laughed. "Oh, no, you're not putting me in that position."

"What position?"

"You'll be mad if I say the wrong thing, which I will most definitely do because there is no right answer."

"What if I promise not to get mad?"

"Okay, if you really want to play this game..." I licked my lips as I eyed her up and down and leaned in, all serious-like. *"Hot as fuck and ready to suck."*

Her jaw clenched, but I could see she was trying not to laugh. "You're a butthole and absolutely no help."

I shrugged. "I told you I wasn't going to answer."

She sighed. "I guess you did." She shook her pen back and forth while she thought.

I was getting bored, so I plucked the pen from her fingers and slid the notecard in front of me.

SUCCESSFUL BUSINESSWOMAN, INTELLIGENT, AND BEAUTIFUL, PRU WORKS IN EVENT PLANNING AND KNOWS ALL THE BEST SPOTS. YOU CAN'T GO WRONG WITH HER AS YOUR DATE. YOU'LL TAKE HER OUT, BUT SHE'LL TAKE YOU UP.

I slid the card back to her. "For someone who's in your line of work and good at her job, I would have thought this would be easy for you."

She stared at the card. "This is really good."

"Pru."

She looked up at me.

"Did you really have any doubts?"

She rolled her eyes and turned her attention to over my shoulder. "Incoming," she whispered.

I turned around to see Dawn walking up to me, waving her small white paper.

"Want to see what I have?"

I shrugged. "Sure." She handed it to me, and I read, "*Meet Dawn. She's blonde and beautiful, and any date with her will not disappoint.*" I gave it back to her. "Sounds good. I'm sure you'll get lots of bids."

She smiled coyly. "Too bad you can't be one of them."

This wasn't going to be fun, but I needed to let her

know I wasn't interested in her. "Yeah, it's probably for the best. I came here with Pru."

Her jaw dropped. "I thought you were single."

"I am, but..."

She smiled kindly. "I get it. You'd rather bid on her."

"I never said that."

"You didn't have to."

Bidding wasn't exactly the verb I'd use when it came to what I wanted to do with Pru.

"Well, I'm going to go mingle in hopes that I find someone who does want to spend some money to have a date with me."

"I'm sure you'll succeed."

Dawn walked away, and I found Pru, who had gone to talk to her friends. Her back was to me, and I wanted to slide up behind her, slip an arm around her waist, and kiss her neck. But I didn't lay a finger on her.

Marissa rushed over just as I reached Pru's side.

"Uh..." Marissa said, wringing her hands. "I'm sorry, but my—"

"*Pru*." A guy who looked to be in his early twenties with glasses that were too big for his face came up behind Marissa, pushed her out of the way, and pulled Pru into his arms. "It's so good to see you."

Pru smiled stiffly as she patted the guy on the arm with the tips of her fingers and didn't hug him back.

"Who's this?" I whispered to Marissa, who had ended up beside me.

She sighed. "My little brother. He's had a crush on Pru

since the two of us were in college and he was still in middle school. And even though she has never been interested in him, he still has grand illusions that she'll go out with him someday."

I could see the resemblance to Manny now that she'd told me that, and I kind of felt bad for the kid.

Pru squirmed away. "It's nice to see you again, Ben." She shot a look to Marissa that had *help me* written all over it.

Ben was oblivious.

I maneuvered my body in front of Pru's and held out my hand. "Hello. I'm Sebastian."

Ben looked up at me. "Whoa." He swallowed. "Are you Pru's boyfriend?"

"No. Just a friend."

Ben's smile returned. "A friend of Pru's is a friend of mine."

Is this kid for real?

"Ben, Dad needs you," Marissa said.

"He does? I didn't hear him call my name."

"Well, he did."

Ben shot finger guns at Pru. "I'll be back."

She laughed awkwardly. If I had to guess, Pru did not want him to come back.

"I'm so sorry," Marissa said as soon as Ben walked away. "I didn't think he was coming, and I specifically left your name out of the list of people who were going to be here." She groaned. "I just know he's going to bid on you."

It looked like Pru wasn't going to have to worry about a

serial killer or a guy who hadn't showered for a week. She was going to have to deal with a schoolboy crush.

"Attention, everyone," Manny said. "It's time to start the bachelorette auction."

The room erupted in cheers, and Pru grabbed Marissa's arm.

"Please ask your dad to put me first."

She nodded and took off for her dad.

"Why do you want to go first?" I asked Pru. I would have thought she'd want to put it off as long as possible.

"Because it's more likely that someone else will bid on me. If I wait until the end, everyone will already have their dates."

"I guess that makes sense. Too bad you told me I couldn't bid on anyone."

Chapter Twelve

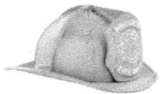

PRU

I WHIPPED my head around to look at Sebastian. Would he actually bid on me if I hadn't told him he couldn't participate?

Manny jumped up onto the small stage that had been set up for the auction with a microphone in his hand. He pushed his palm in a downward motion. "If everyone can quiet down, I'd like to go over the rules."

As the voices dimmed, I grew more nervous. I really didn't want to go on a date with Ben. I wished he would just figure out that I wasn't interested in him.

"Rule number one: all bids start at twenty-five dollars. You can go up in increments in full dollar amounts as small as one dollar to as high as you want." Manny put up two fingers. "Rule two: the auction participant will choose the date if you are the highest bidder. The date can start tonight or be within the next two weeks. The ladies have promised not to drag the date out, but they get to choose when and where. And, fellas, it goes without saying that if they don't want to do anything more than sit and talk to you, you'd best accept it. If any one of my daughter's friends tells me one of you did something inappropriate, I'm going to break both your arms, and then I'm calling the police. Do you understand me?"

There was clapping in the crowd, and some of Marissa's friends shouted their praises.

Someone yelled, "Marissa, your dad is the shit."

For a few moments, I forgot about Ben and the rest of the auction.

Manny grinned and raised the microphone back to his mouth. "If you didn't know, all the money tonight will go to my beautiful wife, Helena's, recovery"—more cheers— "and my equally as beautiful daughter, Marissa, and her future husband for their honeymoon. If you don't have money to spend on the auction, I'm thankful for anything you have to give even if you can only buy a beer tonight."

When everyone finished clapping for what felt like the fifth time, I could no longer put off the inevitable of Ben bidding on a date with me.

"Let's get started, folks," Manny said.

Marissa approached him with the stack of notecards. She turned around to me and gave me two thumbs-up. I took that to mean my card was on the top, and I felt a little relief.

Manny held up the cards. "I have the participants right here. Are you ready?"

"*Yes,*" the crowd yelled.

"All right, let's get started," Manny said. And dropped the notecards on the stage. "Oh crap," he muttered. "Give me a minute, folks, to pick these up."

"You're fucked," Sebastian said.

I scowled at him. "It's not hopeless yet. Marissa told him I wanted to go first." I didn't know if I was saying it more for him or me.

Manny picked up the cards. "The first participant is Isabelle." He looked out into the crowd. "Isabelle, are you here?"

"You were saying?" Sebastian said.

"Shut up."

Isabelle and Elizabeth were a few feet in front of me, and when Isabelle went to the front, Elizabeth watched her with the saddest longing I had ever seen.

I stepped forward and put my arm through Elizabeth's. "Hey, are you okay?" I tilted my head, hoping that Elizabeth would open up to me.

She bit her lip but nodded her head. "Yes, I'm fine."

I sighed. "Just bid on her tonight."

Elizabeth's eyes rounded. "What?"

"Bid on Isabelle."

"Why would I do that?"

I shook my head with exasperation. "Because you like her. As more than a friend."

Elizabeth gasped. "How did you know?"

"Because I have eyes."

She looked around. "Does anyone else know?"

"You mean, our friends? I don't think so, but it's

my job to be observant and pay attention to things. But even if they did, I don't think they would judge you."

"I don't know. I don't know if Isabelle even feels that way about me."

"You won't know until you try."

"What about when it's my turn to go up there?"

"I'll tell Marissa to tell Manny you've changed your mind."

I could practically see the wheels turning in Elizabeth's head.

"Are you sure I should do this?"

"Yes. You have nothing to lose. If Isabelle isn't interested, she'll think you're doing it as a fun joke or to be a good friend or something."

By this time, Manny had finished introducing Isabelle and started the bids. Elizabeth was going to lose her chance if she didn't go for it.

Without a second thought, I whipped my friend's hand up into the air. "One hundred dollars."

Elizabeth's jaw dropped.

"What? You're good for it." I nudged her when she continued to stare at me. "Look at the stage."

Isabelle's expression was somewhere between crying and beaming, and I knew I'd done the right thing.

I watched as a few more people raised their hands, but Elizabeth didn't let that stop her. She finished at two hundred thirty-five dollars.

When Isabelle walked off the stage, she stood in front

of Elizabeth. "You just bid over two hundred dollars to go on a date with me."

Elizabeth blushed. "I did. Is that okay?"

"If you had asked, you could have had one for free."

I made a squeak of happiness and covered my mouth with my hands.

My friends looked at me.

"Ignore me. I'm just so happy."

I didn't even care if I had to go out with Ben. This was the best night I'd ever had.

Although I stepped away to give the two women privacy to talk, I couldn't take my eyes off of them. They were going to make such a cute couple if everything worked out for them.

And suddenly, I realized I was the last friend left of our so-called man-hating group. I supposed someone had to be, but I hadn't thought everyone would find someone so fast. I had often heard that people found someone when they stopped looking, but I hadn't thought it was so true.

"Please welcome Elizabeth," came through the speakers.

Elizabeth twirled around and looked at me.

"Oh, right." That was my cue to say something. "Elizabeth has to withdraw. I'm sorry," I yelled toward the stage.

"No problem," Manny said and flipped to the next card. "We only have two participants left, which brings us to the woman who came up with this idea—Pru from Essence Events."

What? It's my turn already?

I hadn't been paying close enough attention. I had missed all of Marissa's friends.

I gave Sebastian one last glance, giving him a *do I have to do this* look.

He grinned and nodded. *If you don't do it, I don't do it*, he mouthed.

Fine, I mouthed back and headed to the stage.

"*Successful businesswoman, intelligent, and beautiful, Pru works in event planning and knows all the best spots. You can't go wrong with her as your date. You'll take her out, but she'll take you up*," Manny said, reading off the card.

When I reached the stage, I understood why Sebastian didn't want to be up on one. Everyone was staring at me. I knew that it was part of the deal, but it was hard not to feel like a specimen being studied.

Despite being uncomfortable, I smiled and waved. Thankfully, people in the crowd smiled back, and it eased my anxiety.

But as I swept the room, looking for who I might be interested in having bid on a date with me, I saw Ben. He was sitting on the edge of his chair, looking like an excited puppy waiting for a treat.

I groaned. I thought a serial killer might be better than Ben. At least I wouldn't care about breaking a murderer's heart. But poor Ben was still young, and I understood what it was like to have a crush on someone older than you, especially back when I had been around his age.

I just hoped one of these other guys came through

because I did not want to tell Ben I didn't like him like that. I mean, he should have already known, but it seemed like he'd never figure it out.

"Which one of you wants a date with Pru?" Manny said. "The bidding starts at twenty-five dollars."

Someone other than Ben raised his hand. The man was probably older than me, but he looked nice.

"Twenty-five dollars." Manny pointed at him.

"Thirty dollars," someone else yelled, and I began to perk up.

I might actually get a nice date out of this event. Man Two looked closer to my age, and while he wasn't the most handsome, I would be happy to go on a date with him.

Man One and Man Two went back and forth, getting up to fifty dollars. I was getting entirely too comfortable because I had forgotten about Ben—until he bid one hundred dollars, and I realized he'd been waiting until he thought the two guys wouldn't go any higher.

Man One bid one hundred ten, but when Manny pointed to Man Two, he shook his head. The realization that I was going on a date with Ben became more apparent as he and Man One went back and forth.

There was no way the other guy wanted to go on a date with me as much as Ben did.

I looked at Marissa and then Isabelle and Elizabeth. They all looked like they were constipated, which probably meant they had come to the same conclusion I had.

My gaze then traveled over to Sebastian. He was sitting on a stool, leaning back against the bar with both elbows resting there. It seemed he was feeling relaxed without a care in the world and had no idea about the plight I was in. Until I met his eyes. He met mine dead on, and I wanted to punch the smirk off his face. He was enjoying this.

As Ben and the other man were nearing two hundred fifty, I began to panic, and my brain scrambled over ideas of what I was going to do when this was over. It felt like my vision was narrowing when out of nowhere, there was a loud crash at the back of the bar behind the staff doors.

Everyone froze for a moment, and Manny jumped off the stage as he dropped the microphone.

It screeched, and I winced since I was so close to the speakers up front.

Marissa hurried over and picked up the microphone. "We'll take a brief break. Thanks for your patience." She set it down gentler than her dad had and went to follow him to see what had happened.

When I realized that Ben had gone to help too, I saw my chance.

No one was paying me much mind now that I was by myself, and most people had picked up their phones or started talking to their neighbors. Once they realized they couldn't see the cause of the crash and it wasn't an emergency since no one was screaming to call 911, they had turned their attention elsewhere.

I scrambled down the steps to where Sebastian had been sitting since the last time I'd looked at him. He seemed unfazed by the noise in the back room.

"There were a lot of *shits* and *goddammits* back there.

It seems like someone dropped something," he said, as if he'd read my mind. He lifted his chin. "What are you doing over here?"

"Is that your beer?" I nodded toward the bottle next to him.

"Yes."

I picked it up and took several deep swallows, to the point that I had to wipe my mouth with the back of my hand.

"You're welcome," Sebastian said as I set it back down.

"Thanks. I need you to do something for me."

"And what's that?" he asked, eyeing me skeptically.

"I need you to bid on me and outbid Ben."

Sebastian shifted to the side and picked up the beer I had just stolen sips from. "No can do. You told me I couldn't participate."

I ground my teeth together, wondering if I should tell him the truth. Knowing what I knew about Sebastian, I probably didn't have a choice. "I only said that because of Dawn."

His expression didn't change, which meant he'd probably already known. "And why did you say that because of Dawn?"

"Do I have to answer?"

"Yep."

The asshole was really going to make me say it.

"I was jealous." I lifted my hands, waved them back and forth in a mocking manner, and let them fall back to my sides with a slap. "Happy now?"

He didn't gloat like I'd thought he would. He just said, "Ask me again."

"Ask what?"

"The question you came over here to ask."

I took a deep breath. "Will you outbid Ben for me?"

"On one condition."

"Really?" Hadn't he made me jump through enough hoops already?

He shrugged.

"Fine," I said, exasperated. "What's the condition?"

He crooked his finger at me, and when I moved closer, he snagged me around the waist, pulling my body flush against his.

With his mouth against my ear, he said, "If I do this, I'm taking you home and fucking you tonight."

The air left my lungs, and I tried to look at him, but he squeezed me tighter and rubbed his hard length between my legs.

"Yes or no, Pru? Are you going to let me fuck you?"

I was already wet, and it really wasn't worth fighting against. With a simple nod, I gave in and admitted that I wanted him.

"Good girl." He nipped my earlobe and stepped back. "Now, get your ass back up there, so I can claim it as mine."

Chapter Thirteen

SEBASTIAN

I HAD to adjust my cock in my jeans as I watched Pru walk away. I couldn't wait to get her naked, and I didn't know if I was more excited to see what it felt like to be inside her or what it felt like to have her come all over me.

I guessed I would find out soon, but I needed to take care of this auction thing first.

Manny and his two children came out from the back as Pru reached the stage. He held up his hands and said, "Everything's okay, folks. Just a little spill."

I walked over to the table Ben had been sitting at before the back-room incident and waited for him.

When he arrived at the table, he hesitated a moment when he saw me, but then he smiled.

"Everything okay back there?" I asked.

"Oh, yeah. Some plates and glasses got broken, but that's it."

"That's good."

"Is everyone ready to pick up where we left off?" Manny asked.

The crowd answered with a lot of yelling.

I leaned closer to Ben. "Do you know that other guy who is bidding on Pru?"

His mouth formed into a thin line as his eyes drifted to his competition. "No. And I wish he'd stop. I really want to take Pru out."

"Do I hear two hundred seventy-five?" Manny asked, and Ben put up his hand.

"Do you think that's what she wants?" I asked Ben as Pru shot me a look. "I know you've known her a long time, yet you've never gone out before." I put up a finger to Pru. I would get around to keeping my end of the deal.

Ben frowned, as if he'd never thought about what Pru wanted before.

Jesus. I really hoped he realized that relationships went both ways. If not now, someday.

But I hadn't come over here to school Ben. I had come for other information.

"Three hundred," the other guy shouted.

"So, how much money do you have to bid? Do you think you have more than that guy?"

"I only have five hundred. Six at the most."

"Pssh. I'm sure that guy will stop before that amount."

Ben's eyes lit up. "You think so?"

"I sure do."

Ben chewed on his lip, deep in thought, before raising his hand. "Five hundred dollars."

Someone at a nearby table gasped, and Pru's eyes filled with panic.

The other guy shook his head. "I'm out," he said and sat down.

Manny looked at his son.

Ben looked so excited that I almost felt bad about what I was going to do next.

"Five hundred dollars. Going once, going twice—"

"One thousand dollars," I called out.

The crowd quieted for a moment, and then I got some claps and whistles.

"Okay," Manny said. "One thousand dollars. Going once, going twice...and the winner is the handsome gentleman standing next to my son."

Ben turned to me. "You tricked me."

"Come up here, Sebastian, and meet your date." Manny laughed. "But I guess you already know her."

I tilted my head in response to Ben. "How so?"

"You asked me how much money I had, so you could outbid me."

I shook my head. "I was going to do that no matter what."

He pursed his lips. "How do you even know she wants to go out with you?"

Trying to use my logic against me wasn't going to work.

"Because she's already planning to come home with

me tonight." I slapped my hand down on his shoulder. "Sorry, kid."

I strode up to the stage to claim my prize.

When I reached Pru, I put my hand out, and she put her palm in mine. I helped her jump down. As soon as she landed at my feet, I yanked her into my arms and kissed her.

Her lips parted, and I swept my tongue inside. She rubbed hers up against mine and then sucked on my tongue. My groin tightened, and I imagined her doing the same to my dick as I groaned into her mouth. When I pulled away, I snagged her bottom lip between my teeth and licked the inside before letting go.

The crowd cheered for us, and she sighed. "Wow."

"If you think that's exciting, just wait until I'm inside you later."

With her back to the crowd, she discreetly slid her hand between us, down to my front, and cupped me. "I can't wait."

"So, Pru, does this mean you are taking this gentleman out on a date tonight?" Manny asked.

I answered for her, "No, we're going to do that some other time."

"Date's not tonight, folks," Manny told the crowd.

There were a couple of *ahh*s of disappointment, but for the most part, the people probably didn't really care.

Pru looked at me, eyebrows raised. "Oh, we are, are we? What's tonight then?"

"Fucking." I rubbed my thumb over her lower lip. "Fucking's not a date, honey." I looked over at Ben. "I think you should go say something to the kid though. He looks heartbroken."

She took a deep breath and headed over to Ben. I followed behind as his dad called the next participant to the stage.

"Hey, Ben," Pru said when we reached him. "Thanks for bidding on me, and sorry it didn't work out. You're a nice guy."

I winced. She'd totally friend-zoned the guy. Yeah, he should have known, but I still felt for him.

Ben lowered his head before glancing back up. "Thanks."

Pru put her hand on his upper arm. "You'll meet someone perfect for you someday."

She was making it worse.

I grabbed her hand. "Come on, Pru. Your friends are waiting for us."

While Elizabeth and Isabelle were watching us, I didn't know if they were exactly waiting to talk to Pru, but I needed to get her away from Ben before she crushed his whole spirit.

As we headed toward her friends, Marissa met us there with her hands on her hips. "I thought you weren't together?"

"We aren't," we both said.

"I only asked him to bid on me, so your brother wouldn't win a date," Pru explained.

Marissa wrinkled her nose and glimpsed down at our hands. She glanced back up. "Then, why are you holding hands? Hmm?"

We let go immediately.

"That was also for your brother," Pru said. "It's all for show."

Marissa raised her chin. "Right."

"And that is the final bachelorette, folks," Manny said. "Except for one special participant. I'd like to welcome my daughter, Marissa, up here."

Marissa's jaw dropped open as her eyes went to her dad and then to Pru.

Pru put her hands up. "I didn't have anything to do with this." She leaned closer to me. "But it serves her right for giving us crap." She said it loud enough for Marissa to hear, and I had to laugh as Marissa narrowed her eyes at Pru's evil grin.

Marissa dragged her feet on her way up to the stage, and she stopped to speak to her father. We couldn't hear what was said, but it appeared they had a back-and-forth before she reluctantly agreed to get up on the platform.

"All right, everyone, as you know, my daughter's fiancé has been out of the country for what feels like years, and she hasn't been on a date in a long time. I thought maybe one of you could treat her to a fun night out."

Marissa's jaw was practically on the floor. "Dad," she yelled loud enough for us to hear. "I'm not pimping myself out for honeymoon money."

Manny ignored her. "Are we ready to start the bidding?"

"I don't think so." Marissa marched over and went for the microphone.

Manny whipped it out of her reach. "Let's start the bid at one day."

This had everyone pausing since the bidding was usually in dollars.

From the back of the bar, a voice called out, "I bid the rest of my life."

Marissa gasped and jumped off the stage, running to the man who'd spoken. He was wearing a military uniform, and one didn't have to be a genius to see that this was her future husband. Marissa leaped into his arms and wrapped her legs around his waist.

The cheers coming from the crowd were practically deafening, but I didn't blame them. We all needed a feel-good story every now and then.

"Oh my God," Pru said. "They surprised her. He wasn't supposed to come home until next week."

I shifted around to look at her.

She had a hand on her chest, and her eyes glistened with tears.

I wrapped my arm around her and brought my lips to her ear. "I would have never pegged you as a romantic."

She leaned back and scowled at me. "I'm not. I'm just happy for my friend, is all." She inched closer until our lips almost touched. "Besides, you're the one who said we're going on a date later. I was happy with just tonight."

I grabbed the back of her head and tugged her close again. "Once you've had a taste of me, you're going to want more than one night," I warned.

She clicked her tongue, and I imagined the smirk on her face. "We'll see about that."

"Well then, let's get the fuck out of here."

Chapter Fourteen

PRU

"WOULD YOU LIKE SOMETHING TO DRINK?"

I followed Sebastian into the kitchen. "Sure."

He opened the fridge and pulled out two beers. After twisting off the top, he handed one to me and leaned back against the counter to open his own bottle.

I hopped up onto the island and took a long drink. "So, how long were you living in Indianapolis?"

"Seven years."

"Why'd you move there?"

He shrugged. "Something different."

"And why did you move back?"

"My parents are getting older. I'm an uncle now. I wanted to be closer to my family."

I took another drink. "I vaguely remember your sister from when I was little." I couldn't quite remember her name though. I tilted my head to the side. "You probably didn't throw frogs at her."

He chuckled. "I probably did worse."

"Probably?"

"There was the one time I stole her favorite Barbie and cut off the hair."

My jaw dropped, and I laughed.

"To be fair, she had just told my mom that I was peeing behind the shed in our backyard. She had it coming to her for being a tattletale."

"Did you get punished for your outdoor bathroom use?"

He smiled. "Nah. My dad just told me to never do it again."

"And you still cut off Barbie's hair?"

"Snitches gets stitches. Or in that case, haircuts." He lifted his bottle to his lips and took several swallows before setting his beer down and walking the few feet that separated us. "But you didn't come here to talk to me about my sister."

Shaking my head, I admitted, "No, I didn't."

And knowing that the good stuff was about to happen next, I put my drink to my lips once more. It had been a while since I'd let myself have sex, and I needed the liquid courage.

As I raised my chin to wash down that last bit of anxiety, Sebastian kissed my neck.

I closed my eyes as he licked on the sensitive skin there. I was so aroused that I was already wet, and I might have whimpered as I drew the bottle away.

He moved his face around to mine. "Why don't you let

me take that before you spill it? I don't need you making two messes in my kitchen," he said as he took my beer and set it down behind him.

"Two messes?" I asked.

But rather than answer me, Sebastian kissed me. Immediately, I wrapped my arms around his neck and dug my nails into his upper back.

His tongue slipped inside my mouth, and I slid mine along his. Tilting my head, I gave him better access. He was slow and thorough, and the unhurriedness of it only made it that much better.

At some point, Sebastian pulled away and yanked off his shirt.

Faced with a muscular chest from hours of firefighting and training, I couldn't resist touching him. Some women liked hair on a man, but I loved feeling all his smooth skin. Except for the dark trail that led from his belly button to the promised land. I didn't need an arrow pointing to a man's dick, but it didn't hurt. I licked my lips as I ran my hands all over his torso. For someone so strong and masculine, his skin was soft. I could touch him for days.

Sebastian groaned and took my mouth again. This time with a little more urgency. His lips soon left mine and trailed down my throat and over my sternum until he reached the top of my breasts that my shirt didn't cover.

I sucked in a breath, and that must have been all the encouragement he needed because in the next second, my top was gone.

He yanked down one strap of my bra and drew a

nipple into his mouth. He sucked on the tip and rubbed his tongue on the underside while his facial hair scraped my tender skin.

I clutched the back of his head at the contrasting sensations. "Oh God, that feels amazing."

When he released my now-throbbing nip, he moved over to my other breast and gave it the same treatment as he laid me back on the counter. The surface was cold, but the difference between that and Sebastian's hot skin made me more aware of every tingle in my body.

Sebastian slid his hand underneath my back, and with a flick of his fingers, my bra was undone. He drew it off my arms and threw it somewhere as he kissed down my belly to my pants.

Once he reached them, he quickly had them unbuttoned, and he grabbed the sides. "Lift," he demanded, and I arched my back.

No more than three seconds later, I was naked on Sebastian Creed's kitchen counter like a buffet for him to sample.

With my heels on the edge of said counter, he ran a finger through my lips, so I let my legs fall to the sides. I peeked through my open knees to watch him. Using one hand, he attacked his own jeans while he pushed a thumb inside me with the other.

He grunted, and I wasn't sure what that response meant, but when he dragged the wet digit up and over my clit, I didn't care.

I closed my eyes as he made small circles over my hard

nub. Soon, I started rotating my hips, seeking a non-self-induced orgasm.

The sound of Sebastian's jeans hitting the floor and the disappearance of his hand had my eyes flying open. A condom wrapper from I didn't know where was being ripped open and tossed aside, and the remaining rubber was placed on the head of his shaft.

I lifted my head. "I want to see." I wanted to know if Sebastian's confidence had anything to do with what he was packing.

"Later," he said, grabbing my hips and yanking my ass to the edge. With one hard thrust, he drove inside of me.

"*Goddammit,*" I yelled, spreading my fingers wide against the counter. "You could have warned me you were so big."

He grunted again without a hint of a smile at the compliment I had just given him. "Do you want me to pull out?"

"Don't you fucking dare." I breathed deeply to let my body loosen up. "Just go nice and—"

The air was pulled from my lungs as he picked me up. My arms went around his neck as he carried me over to one of his island stools. His hands were underneath my ass as he sat, keeping me a few centimeters away.

Gently, he lowered me the rest of the way down. "Relax."

It was hard to do when his cock was now farther in me than it had been before. But this wasn't my first time straddling a man, and I knew he was right, so I untensed and let myself adjust to him.

He kissed my neck. "Good girl," he said, running his hands up and down my naked back. "Now, I want you to ride me."

I bit his shoulder. "What if I don't want to?" But I wanted to. Oh, did I want to.

"Listen, I can stay inside you all night, but you're not getting off this dick until you come."

God. Why did he have to call my bluff with his sexy fucking mouth?

All the while, "this dick" stretched me in all the right places. He filled me full, and I honestly couldn't wait to see how it felt when I moved.

"You don't fight fair."

"Honey, I'm trying to give you an orgasm. What's fair got to do with it?" Fingers grasping the back of my neck, he plunged his tongue into my mouth. He had me rocking my hips before he released my lips.

I quickened my pace, finding the bars on the side of the stool to grip my feet against them so I could ride Sebastian hard. This was really the best position for his cock to hit my G-spot, and I was already seeing stars. I didn't want to come yet though. It had been so long since I'd had good sex, and when it was over, it would be over.

Sebastian grabbed my ass, lifting me up and sliding me back down a few times. "I know you're holding out on me."

"No...you...don't," I panted.

"Oh yeah?" He grinned at me. "Come," he said, jerking me down until I couldn't go any further.

"*Fuck*," I yelled as my legs started to shake, and it traveled up the rest of my body.

The stars I had seen earlier disappeared as blackness filled my vision and my hearing dimmed. All my senses narrowed in on the orgasm that flooded my body while Sebastian held me.

"Oh God," I sighed and let go of all my muscles.

I fell back onto his hands, and my arms dangled by my sides. I had no more strength.

Sebastian lifted me onto the counter once more and grabbed my hips as he started thrusting.

I arched my back because now that I had climaxed, I was sensitive, and watching him bite his lip as he took me was incredibly hot.

He slowed down but slammed into me forcefully, not once or twice, but a third time, before he cranked his neck back and let go.

A drop of sweat fell from his chin onto my abdomen, and I rubbed it around, as if to absorb this moment and him.

When he looked down at me, he stared for a second without a word before hauling me into his arms and walking out of the kitchen. He was still inside me, and every step had him hitting some secret spots all over again.

"Where are we going?" I asked.

"My bedroom."

We entered the same room I had spent the night in a couple of weeks ago. He laid me on the bed and pulled out.

"Wow," I whispered. I couldn't believe how empty I felt.

Sebastian pulled the condom off and used an article of clothing he'd grabbed from his bed to wipe himself off. He took my hand and placed it around his still-hard cock. "Is this what you wanted?"

He was long and thick. I glanced up at him and nodded. The man was blessed.

He let me play and explore while he tied the end of the condom, but all too soon, he grasped my wrist and pulled it away.

"I'll be back." He went to his bathroom, presumably to throw away the rubber, and came back in, still naked.

His dark trail really did lead to a treasure. I hadn't had an orgasm like that in a long time. Years even.

Sebastian slid onto the bed next to me and pulled me into his arms. He flicked a nipple with his thumb and sucked it into his mouth.

I made a noise, and he lifted his head.

"You didn't think we were done, did you?"

Chapter Fifteen

PRU

THE SOUND OF "BEFORE HE CHEATS" by Carrie Underwood blasted through my subconscious, waking me up from a heavy sleep.

It was Bree. Because of my job, I had given my family and close friends their own ringtones, so if my generic ring sounded and it was after hours, I wouldn't answer it in case it was work.

I pushed the covers off my head as I fully woke up, and I realized that I was still naked in Sebastian's bed.

Hmm. I was surprised I'd slept all night because I was used to sleeping alone. If I did sleep with someone, I wanted him on his side of the bed while I stayed on mine.

I picked up my phone, trying to remember when I had brought it to the bedroom but was drawing a blank. "Hello?" My voice was hoarse. I grimaced.

"Good morning, sunshine."

"Morning." I lifted the covers and peeked underneath.

There was a nice taut ass, which meant Sebastian was wearing as much clothing as me.

"Uh-oh, did the auction not work out last night? Is that why you didn't call? Or did you have a late night?"

Crap. I'd forgotten I was going to call Bree, and wouldn't she like to know about last night? I didn't know if you could consider going to bed at a reasonable time but being up every few hours for sex a late night.

How did I let myself get in this situation?

I slid back under the comforter and winced. Sebastian and his big dick had given me a sore pussy. I was tempted to poke him in the back and make it hurt even though my pain was minimal.

"Pru?"

I'd zoned out. "Sorry, the auction went well."

Sebastian shifted on the bed and rolled over.

"Who bid on you?" Bree asked.

The naked man staring at me.

Okay, I needed to make this nonchalant. I couldn't make it a big deal, but I also couldn't make it too casual, or she'd be suspicious.

"Sebastian," I answered.

"*My cousin?*" Bree asked, shocked.

Her cousin, who pulled the covers over his head.

"Yes, that Sebastian."

He lifted my leg that was closest to him and moved between my thighs.

"But he did it because I'd asked him to. Ben was there."

"Who's that?" Bree asked.

Sebastian's warm mouth landed on my pussy, and I flinched at the sudden touch.

"Marissa's little brother, who's had a crush on me since I met him."

Sebastian's tongue gently circled my clit, and I had to bite my lip, so I wouldn't whimper.

"And?" Bree prompted.

"And he was bidding on me."

Circle. Flick. Suck.

"What's wrong?" Bree asked, and I realized I must have made a noise.

"Nothing," I said a little too quickly. I shoved my hand under the sheets and grabbed on to Sebastian's hair. I rotated my hips against his mouth. "Anyway, I didn't want to break his heart, so I had to bribe your cousin to outbid Ben."

I raised the phone away from my mouth because I could no longer breathe normally.

"What did you bribe him with?"

"Huh?"

Bree chuckled. "Are you okay?"

Well, considering your sexy cousin is about this close *to making me come, I think I'm doing great.*

"Just tired," I squeaked out as a climax racked my body. I bit my tongue so hard that I drew blood so that I didn't give myself away.

"Well, what did you bribe Sebastian with?" Bree asked again as the very person she was inquiring about slithered up my body.

He snatched the phone from my hand. "Pru's going to have to call you back."

I heard Bree gasp just before he hit End, and he dropped my phone as he pushed inside me. Flinging my arms around him, I clutched at his back as he began to fuck me for what had to be about the fifth time since last night.

My phone rang on the floor.

We both ignored it.

———

"Where the hell is my shirt?" I asked the empty kitchen as I searched every crevice. I had already found my underwear, my jeans, and my bra, but my shirt was hiding.

I did another circle of the island before I found it.

I finger-combed my hair and went back into Sebastian's bedroom. He was on his stomach, and his eyes were closed, so I turned right back around.

"Leaving without saying good-bye?"

I twirled. "I thought you were sleeping."

He rolled onto his back. "Nope. I'm awake." He shifted up until he was leaning against the headboard, and the covers fell down to his lap. His chest was just as impressive in the daylight as it had been the night before.

"Thanks for last night."

"Which part?" he asked with a smirk.

"The *bidding on me* part," I purposely said.

Sebastian laughed and made the *okay* sign with his hand with a mocking smile. "Got it."

It was hard to forget that same mouth had gone down on me this morning after we had sex all night. Apparently, Sebastian did not shy away from giving head to a woman.

I got shivers.

Time to refocus. "You're going to do the Date with a Firefighter auction, right?"

"Hmm." He tilted his head back and forth, as if he was thinking.

I stepped forward. "You and I made a deal—"

Sebastian started laughing. "Relax, Pru. I was joking."

I took in a deep breath and exhaled, so I could resist the impulse to tackle him for messing with me.

"On that note, I'm going home. I need to shower and do some work today."

His eyes skimmed down my body and back up. "Too bad. I think you're good just the way you are."

I shook my head. "Good-bye, Sebastian," I said and spun around to leave.

"Tell Bree I said hi," he yelled once I was outside his bedroom.

I pulled my phone from my pocket and slid my heels on at the door.

Three missed calls.

I groaned. Maybe I didn't have to call her back right away. It wasn't like she was going to track me down or anything.

Chapter Sixteen

PRU

THE WATER LAPPED my clavicle as I shifted in the bathtub. When I'd arrived home from Sebastian's, I'd decided to treat myself to a hot bath rather than rushing through a shower.

I only had a birthday party I had to take care of for work this afternoon. I pretty much had to make sure the decorations were up and the cake was delivered. Things the hostess could easily do herself, but since she would rather pay me to do it, I'd happily oblige.

I loved doing complex events like weddings or the firemen fundraiser, but the occasional easy event, like a birthday or anniversary party, made my job a little less stressful.

Carrie Underwood drifted up from my bathroom floor.

With a sigh, I used a towel to dry off my hands and picked up my cell.

"Hello?"

"Hello? That's all you have to say to me?" Bree said.

"It is the standard phone greeting."

"Whatever. About our conversation earlier this morning."

I tried to stop the smile spreading across my face because I didn't want Bree to hear it. "What about it?"

"You had sex with my cousin."

"I plead the Fifth."

"So, we're just sleeping with our friends' relatives now?" Her tone sounded more perplexed than accusing.

"I was only following your example."

I could just picture Bree narrowing her eyes at me. "It's not the same."

"You're right. Yours was worse. I merely slept with your cousin. You slept with Tessa's brother."

"*Ha.* So, you did have sex with Sebastian."

"You already knew I did."

She chuckled. "I did. But it's still not the same. I love Zack, and we're getting married."

I snorted. "You weren't in love with him when you screwed him."

"Does this mean you're going to fall in love with my cousin?"

I laughed so hard that I started slipping underneath the water. "Don't make me laugh. I almost drowned."

"Hmph. He's not that bad."

"Says you. You're biased."

"Only a little."

"Besides, I'm good as I am. Just me, myself, and I. All

of you might have broken the club rules, but not me. Hmm...I might need to recruit new members."

"You would never. And there's still Isabelle and Elizabeth. Why do you always forget about them?"

Because I could tell that Elizabeth had been in love with Isabelle for a long time. And after last night, something might come of that. But it wasn't my secret to reveal. And I guessed, technically, they were still on board with the *no men* part.

"Well, Elizabeth hasn't dated anyone for years, so she can stay in the club with me." *Hello?* We all should have realized she wasn't into men years ago. "But while Isabelle is single now, she was dating a guy for a while. Just because they broke up doesn't mean she didn't already break the rules."

"Yeah, yeah, you have a point. Speaking of Isabelle and Elizabeth, how did last night go for them?"

Oh shit. I didn't know what to say about that.

"Good. I have to go though. I'm turning into an icicle in the tub."

Bree sighed. "Okay."

"Bye."

"Bye." She sounded confused.

I felt bad, but I wasn't up for some elaborate lie, so I quickly hit End on my phone and dropped it onto the rug.

———

On Tuesday, I sent Sebastian a text with his choices for catering. I had found a few who were available to do it that I thought would be good for his event.

He messaged me back an hour later.

> Sebastian: You pick. That's why I hired you.

> Me: Are you sure?

I didn't like being the person making the final decision on things and then having clients complain because they didn't like something.

> Sebastian: Would you use one of these companies for your own event?

> Me: I would use any of them.

> Sebastian: Then, I trust you to pick.

> Me: What's Rory's number?

> Sebastian: Why the fuck do you need Rory's number?

> Me: Hostile much? Sheesh.

> Me: If you must know, Rory seems to care more about this than you do. And I want someone from the fire station to give me their input.

Sebastian: Fine. I pick the first one.

I laughed in disbelief.

Me: You're really not going to give me Rory's number?

Sebastian: Nope.

Me: Why?

Sebastian: Because we don't need another Ben situation.

I scoffed at my phone. *How ridiculous.*

Me: Ben was one person. I can guarantee that not everyone gets a crush on me. I mean, I am gorgeous, but not all men want to fuck me.

Sebastian: Not all men, but plenty of them. And no one will be fucking you while I'm fucking you.

Sebastian: You're not getting Rory's number.

This. This right here was why I didn't like alpha men.

Me: Correction: you fucked me. Past tense.

Sebastian: We'll see about that.

Chapter Seventeen

SEBASTIAN

"HOW'S THE PARTY PLANNING COMING?" Rory asked me as he walked into the exercise room at work. It wasn't much, but it had free weights and a treadmill. Working out was something to do on a slow day.

I put down the weights I had been holding and picked up my towel to wipe the sweat from my face. "Good." Except for the fact that I hadn't seen Pru since she'd left my house Sunday morning almost a week ago. And I hadn't heard from her since she'd messaged me about the food on Tuesday. It was Thursday, and I hadn't gotten so much as an email since.

And she still owed me a date.

"Good. That's it?" Rory asked.

"We have a venue and donations for the silent auction, and a theme picked out." Pru had decided the theme was *Hearts on Fire* to represent the foundation we were supporting and because we were firefighters. "I think we have the catering down. I told her to pick a vendor, but she hasn't let me know who we're going with."

Rory's eyes bugged. "You told her to pick one?"

I shrugged. "Yeah."

"What did she say?"

I laughed. "She asked me for your phone number."

He smiled and looked relieved. "That's why she's been messaging me. She set up some times for me to meet her to try out food. I was wondering why she was asking me instead of you, but that explains it." He waved his phone back and forth and headed for the door. "Thank you."

"Stop."

Rory halted at the door at my simple command and pivoted on his heel.

I made a *come* motion with my hand. "Let me see."

I had planned on giving her Rory's number. I'd only been messing with her when I told her no even though I could see Rory totally falling for Pru. But she never responded to my last text and seemed to be avoiding me, so I waited to send her the number. It seemed she had found it herself.

"I don't know if I should do that," Rory said.

"Is there something on there I shouldn't see?"

"Of course not. No. It's just that she trusts me to keep our conversations private."

"Um"—I tapped my chin for emphasis—"she trusts you to keep your conversations private, but then you come in here and tell me about said conversations."

Rory's cheeks slowly turned pink.

"Since I am the one in charge of this fundraiser, I think you should let me see what Pru isn't telling me."

He sighed, knowing I'd won the argument. He unlocked his phone and opened up his messages. Reluctantly, he handed his cell over to me.

> Pru: Hi, Rory. This is Pru. I am the event planner working on the fundraiser for your fire department.

> Rory: I remember you. Hello.

> Pru: Thank you again for asking your coworkers about the auction. I really appreciate it.

> Rory: Your very welcome.

I studied the phone in my hand, surprised it wasn't covered in syrup for all the sweet words these two were piling on each other.

> Pru: I have another favor to ask you if you aren't too busy.

> Rory: Shoot. ☺

> Pru: Sebastian is busy, but I need someone from the department to okay the food category. Would you have time to attend a few tastings?

> Rory: I would love to!

Pru: Excellent. Is there a day that works for you?

Rory: I'm off on Friday.

Friday? That was tomorrow.

Pru: I think I can make Friday work.

Rory: Will you be there? I've never done this before.

I rolled my eyes.

Pru: I will. It's all part of my job description.

Nice, Pru. Way to make sure he knows you'll be there for work.

"Why are you grinning?"

I scowled at Rory. "Shut up and let me finish."

Rory: Good. Just tell me when and where.

Pru: I will get back to you with that.

A couple hours later, Pru had sent another text, listing the places and times. The first two were at one and two thirty in the afternoon. The third was scheduled at four.

Pru: Sorry, it's going to be a busy afternoon.

Rory: That's fine. I'll be there.

Pru: See you then.

I took a screenshot with the locations and times and messaged it to myself. I closed the app and gave the phone back to Rory.

"You're going to go instead of me, aren't you?"

"I am."

"Can I come too?"

I thought about it. "No."

"But I could help."

"I doubt it." I stepped around him and headed for the locker room. "You can't even spell *you're*."

"Huh?" Rory came running after me.

I laughed and shook my head. "*You're welcome* is you are. Y-O-U-apostrophe-R-E."

He didn't respond right away until I heard, "Crap." I took that to mean he'd opened his phone and gone back to his text messages with Pru. "Do you think she noticed?"

"Probably not." *Most definitely.* No way she'd missed that.

When we reached my locker, the look on Rory's face resembled a lost puppy.

"Look, if you want to come, you can."

His face brightened. "Really?"

"Yeah. She did ask you."

He slapped me on the back. "Thanks, Sebastian," he said and started to leave.

"Rory."

He stopped and turned.

I put my finger to my lips. "Don't tell Pru I'm coming tomorrow."

He pulled his hand across his lips like he was zipping up his mouth.

It was a good thing Rory and I had the same day off. Pru was going to be in for a surprise.

Chapter Eighteen

PRU

I TAPPED my fingers on the table and picked up my phone for the tenth time. Rory was cutting it close. I had gotten to the catering place early to speak to the staff, so I had expected to wait, but he was on the verge of being late. I was beginning to regret asking him to step in for Sebastian. Maybe I should have just made a decision on my own.

The door opened, and I stood. But it wasn't Rory who entered. It was Sebastian.

"Hey, sorry I'm late," he said, approaching the table. When he reached me, he kissed me on the cheek and walked over to a seat without another word.

I stared at him, speechless.

"Are we going to sit?" he asked.

"What are you doing here?" I blurted out.

He hadn't wanted to make any decisions on the caterer for the fundraiser, and I purposely hadn't invited him after his domineering Tarzan text messages. Yet here he was, alone.

Poor Rory. He'd been excited about this.

A member of the staff came out of the kitchen then, so I pulled out my chair. Decisions had to be made, no matter who had shown up today.

Sebastian followed my cue and took his seat as the man set a large tray down in front of us with food, a couple of plates, sets of silverware, and napkins.

"These are your appetizer options," the gentleman said. He pointed out each dish. "Let me know if you have any questions." And then he left us to choose between them.

"These look delicious," Sebastian said.

Reluctantly, I handed him a plate, silverware, and a napkin. "They do. You know who would have enjoyed it?"

"Who?" he asked as he loaded different appetizers on his plate without looking at me.

"Who?" I repeated. "Rory would have. He was excited to come."

Sebastian looked up at me and licked his thumb.

It shouldn't have been sexy since I was mad at him, but I knew what he could do with that mouth.

"Rory didn't message you?"

"No."

"He's sick."

I pursed my lips. "I don't believe you."

Sebastian laughed and picked up his phone. After a few seconds, he handed it to me.

Rory: Hey. I can't make it today. I got sick in the middle of the night, and I've had it coming out both ends.

I gagged a little. Not something I wanted to read right before eating.

Sebastian: Shit, that sucks. I could have used your input today.

Rory: Yeah, I'm bummed.

Sebastian: I'll make sure to send you pictures of my favorites. Maybe you can help me decide that way.

Rory: Please don't. Just thinking about food makes me feel like throwing up again.

Sebastian: Got it. I'll save the pictures for when you're feeling better.

Rory: Thanks.

Sebastian: I hope you feel better soon. And don't forget to let Pru know you're not coming today. She might need to make some adjustments.

I tried not to get warm and fuzzy feelings from Sebastian thinking about me since he hadn't told me he was coming in the first place, which was also something that might have required me making adjustments.

Setting his cell down, I asked, "Were you mad that I didn't tell you about the tasting plans?" I hoped his answer would remind me what an overbearing man he could be.

"Hmm." He tilted his head, as if he really had to think about it. "More like irritated that you didn't ask me to come and you were going to go ahead with this anyway. And a little hurt that you had left me out."

A single laugh bubbled up from the back of my throat.

Sebastian met my eyes, his face serious.

"You're joking." I scoffed. "I didn't hurt your feelings." Did alpha males even have feelings?

He looked unimpressed. "I am a human being, you know, and I do have feelings." It was like he had read my mind.

"You told me to pick a place, so I assumed you didn't want to be a part of today. I was wrong." It was the best I was going to give him because I didn't quite believe he wasn't playing with me. I didn't want to tell him I was sorry and have him laugh because I had believed him.

Sebastian's phone rang, and out of habit, I looked down since it was next to me.

The caller ID read *Angela*, and the immediate jealousy that spread through my body pissed me off.

"I'd better get this." Sebastian used his napkin to clean his mouth and answered his phone. "Hello?"

"*Hey, I know you have today off. Are you busy?*" I heard a feminine voice say through the phone.

Was this Angela asking if Sebastian had the day off, so they could meet up for sex?

He looked at me and held up a finger while I gritted my teeth and tried to smile.

————

SEBASTIAN

I found a remote corner, so I could speak to my sister in private. Despite the casual tone she was taking, she didn't normally call me at the last minute and ask me if I was busy. Something had to be up.

"I am working on some stuff for my fire department's fundraiser."

She sighed. "I figured you already had plans. Thanks anyway."

"Wait. What is going on?"

"Ugh. Shelby's day care closed for the rest of the day because of a lice breakout. I already had her checked, and she's clear, but I can't find anyone to take her. I have an important meeting this afternoon, and Luis can't get out of work either. And Mom and Dad are on vacation." She sighed again. "I'll just have to take Shelby with me to work and pray she cooperates."

"Where are you now?"

"I just left the hair place that checked her for lice. I'm about twenty minutes from work."

I smiled. "I don't really have time to pick Shelby up,

but you can bring Shelby to me, and I'll watch her. I'm probably ten minutes out of your way though."

"I don't care," she said before I even finished my last sentence. "Send me the address, and I'll bring her to you. You are a lifesaver."

"Hold on." I sent her the directions, so she could put them in her phone before returning back to the conversation.

"I don't know about lifesaver. I'm just a nice brother-slash-uncle." This was one of the reasons I had moved back to Minnesota, and I was glad I could help my sister out. I just hoped Shelby wouldn't get too bored. "You don't happen to have your iPad for her to play with, do you?"

Angela laughed. "How do you think I was going to keep her occupied during my meeting?"

"Perfect. I'm doing some food tasting today, so Shelby might have fun, helping me, but I like the reassurance of having an iPad in case she gets bored."

My niece was only three and got uninterested in things very easily.

"And tell me again, who checked her for lice and guaranteed she isn't going to give it to me?"

Chapter Nineteen

PRU

SEBASTIAN CAME BACK to the table after almost ten minutes.

I wanted to ask him so many questions. *Who is Angela? Why did you have to speak to her in private? What did you two talk about? Are you going to see her later?*

I groaned at my irrational brain and its onset of thoughts.

"Is something wrong?" Sebastian asked me.

Right. I should have kept my groaning to myself.

"No, everything is good," I fibbed, but I decided to do some prying. "Did Rory tell you all the times we are scheduled for today?" Not wanting to look at him, I grabbed more food off the tray. "Do you need to cancel or reschedule anything?"

"Nope. As long as you don't mind a little company, that is," he said with an endearing smile.

I almost dropped the spoon I was using. *He invited his date here? What an asshole.*

We'd had sex together less than a week ago. I couldn't believe him. If I wasn't there for my job, I would walk out.

I counted to ten, so my voice would be even as I asked, "Who is coming—"

His phone rang again. "Hold that thought." He answered. "Are you here? Okay. I'll meet you out front." He ended his call. "I'll be right back."

I wasn't sure why, but I started to panic. How was I supposed to act around this woman? It seemed silly that I was nervous, but I was afraid I was going to give it away that I'd slept with Sebastian.

I heard Sebastian say something before I could see him, and then I heard a small feminine giggle. I rolled my eyes. I shouldn't be so mean, but I hated it when women bolstered men's egos unnecessarily. They really didn't need it.

At the last second, I grabbed my cell, so I could look like I was busy and not someone waiting anxiously for the guy she liked to come back with another woman.

"Pru?" Sebastian said.

"Yes?" I said as I lifted my head, but I soon trailed off when I saw who was standing next to him. I was completely without words.

"Pru, this is my niece, Shelby. Shelby, this is my friend, Pru."

That explained who Angela was. I felt silly for forgetting his sister's name even if I hadn't seen her in years.

Shelby was adorable with dark hair that was up in pigtails and big brown eyes to match her uncle's.

I smiled. "Hi, Shelby. Did you come to hang out with your uncle this afternoon?"

She nodded. "My day pare have mice."

"Lice," Sebastian corrected at my horrified look.

"I don't think that's any better," I told him.

He put his hands over Shelby's ears. "Don't scare her. Also, my sister already had her checked, and she's cleared."

"Right. Of course." *Thank God.*

He pulled his hands away. "Want to come and sit with Uncle Sebastian and try some food with us?"

Shelby nodded again as her uncle set a pink backpack on the floor.

Sebastian pulled a chair from another table over to ours and put it right next to his, but once he sat his niece down, I couldn't see her face.

I peeked under the table to see her better and smiled. "How old are you?"

Holding up three fingers, she said, "Free."

"Three? Wow, you're so big."

She grinned.

"Shelby's going to be four next month," Sebastian said as he sat in his own chair, which brought his crotch dangerously close to my face.

Why did I neglect to give this man a blow job?

My cheeks heated as I quickly sat up. "How exciting. Are you going to have a birthday party?" I asked Shelby.

She got up on her knees. "Yep. Wiff cake."

"Yum. I like cake."

"Did someone say cake?" our server said as he walked over to us.

"We have an extra taster today," I explained.

"We're just about to bring out the samples for the main courses." He put his hand up to his mouth and whispered, "Do you want me to bring the C-A-K-E out early?"

"No, let's wait. She might get a sugar high, and then I won't know what to do with her," Sebastian said.

The server smiled. "Wise decision."

"Oh. And do you have a booster chair?" I asked before he walked away. I didn't want to find myself staring at Sebastian's crotch again.

———

When we finished with the appetizers, main courses, and dessert, Sebastian took Shelby to the restroom to wash her hands and face. After we walked outside toward the parking lot, Sebastian stopped suddenly, Shelby's hand in his.

"Oh no."

"What's wrong?"

"I don't have a car seat for her. Shit."

"Uncle Bastian, you're not s'posed to say that word," Shelby said as I pulled out my phone.

"Sorry, Shelb. Uncle Sebastian just realized he doesn't have a way to drive you anywhere."

"You have no car?"

"I have a car. I just don't have a seat for you."

"Why not?"

I snorted. *Children.* Their minds were beautifully simple.

"Because I don't have any kids." Sebastian eyed my lower stomach. "Yet."

My mouth fell open. "I don't think so." I took birth control, and we had used condoms.

"Is Pru your girlfwiend?" Shelby asked.

Maybe their minds weren't as simple as I had thought.

Sebastian laughed at what had to be a look of horror on my face. "No, we're just friends."

"Too bad. She's pwetty."

"She is pretty, isn't she?" he said, smiling at me.

"Flattery will normally get you nowhere, but today, it gets you an Uber with a car seat."

"Thank you," Sebastian said.

"You're welcome."

"Shelb, Pru got us a special ride."

"Yay." Shelby clapped her hands.

When the driver arrived, I started for my own car.

"Aren't you going to ride with us?" Sebastian asked as he picked up Shelby and buckled her into the car seat. "There's no point in us taking two vehicles to the next tasting, especially if you're paying for this one."

He had a point, but I kind of needed a Sebastian break. Watching him with his niece did things to my insides.

"Come wiff, Pru," Shelby said.

Sebastian turned to me with puppy-dog eyes. "You're not going to say no to that, are you?"

I sighed and smiled. "I mean, how can I? I'll ride with you."

"Yay," Shelby said again.

"But I'm riding in front," I told Sebastian. I was not going to be squeezed in the back with him, our bodies touching the whole time.

Chapter Twenty

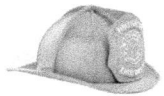

PRU

"I DON'T THINK I could eat another bite," Sebastian said.

"You and me both."

"More cake," Shelby said, and I laughed.

Sebastian looked at her sternly. "No more cake."

Her little lip started to waver as it protruded out.

"Uh-oh," I said under my breath.

We were at our last appointment of the day, and this one was a restaurant that catered. There were people sitting around us that probably didn't want to hear a three-year-old cry.

"But I have your iPad," he said as he yanked it from her backpack.

Shelby's eyes immediately widened, and she beamed. She held out her hands for it, and all signs of crying were gone.

"That was close."

"Electronics are the best at keeping kids occupied. I don't know what our parents did without them."

"Good to know." It was a good tip if I ever had kids someday.

Our server came over at that time. "Is there anything else I can get you?"

"I'll have a beer," Sebastian said.

"Half a glass of wine for me."

"Damn," Sebastian said, eyes on me.

Was he remembering what Marissa said about me and beer? I wasn't about to ask.

"Is something wrong?" the server said as I frowned in confusion.

He looked over at her. "Oh, no. Everything's fine. Forget I said anything."

"One beer and half a glass of wine. And for the little—" The server laughed. "Never mind."

Sebastian and I looked over to see that Shelby had fallen asleep. Her head was on the back of the chair with her mouth open. She was adorable.

"That was fast," I said in amazement.

"That's what happens," the server said knowingly. "I'll be right back with your drinks."

"Hey, now that she's sleeping, we can drink in peace," Sebastian said.

I laughed. "You're so nice."

He just smiled at me.

"What was the *damn* about?"

He shook his head with a chuckle. "Never mind."

I thought about pushing him but figured it might be for the best that I didn't. "So, did you decide on a caterer for the fundraiser?"

He blew out a big breath of air. "They're all good."

I'd seen this before. "Okay, how about we eliminate one? Which did you like the least?"

"Probably the first one."

I nodded in agreement. "Now, you have two left. What do you think people will enjoy more?"

Putting his elbow on the table, he leaned forward. "When I told you to pick one the other day, what was your first pick?"

I raised my eyebrows. "Nice try."

"You're too smart for me."

I scoffed. "Obviously."

"Okay, so the second place was great, and they were a catering place. Number three—this place—is a well-known restaurant. I'm leaning toward this option because people will want to come for the food."

"That is one way to make a decision. But most people are going to come for the fundraiser, not for the food."

"You've worked with both companies more than once?"

"Yes."

"Does one handle bigger crowds more than the other?"

I thought back to the many events I had planned. "No, they're both excellent."

"Dammit, Pru, meet me halfway."

I laughed at him. "Okay, okay. If I had to pick, I would

pick this place." I held up my hand before he could say anything. "But it's for purely selfish reasons."

"Hmm." His gaze traveled up and down. "And what's that?"

"Their salted pretzels." I closed my eyes and licked my lips. "They are so good."

"Fuck, Pru."

I lifted my lids to see Sebastian's hand under the table as he shifted in his seat.

"Sorry." I grinned.

"You are not. You love torturing me."

"I wouldn't say *love*." But I did *like* it.

The server brought our drinks over and quickly disappeared.

I picked up my glass as Sebastian tilted his phone halfway off the table and frowned.

"Is something wrong?"

"I just figured my sister would be here by now to pick up Shelby. She messaged me almost an hour ago that she was getting off work soon."

"Do you think you're stuck with her for the night?"

He shrugged. "I doubt it. I just hope everything is okay."

I sipped my wine. "Why do you assume it's not?"

He chuckled. "Because I'm a firefighter. I've seen shit you've never even thought of."

"That sucks."

"Someone has to do it. And sometimes, we have a happy outcome too."

The only thing I knew about Sebastian's job was what little I saw in the media and in television shows, many of which probably had information wrong.

"Oh, she's here."

I pulled myself from my thoughts as Sebastian set his cell down and stood. But before he could pick up Shelby, a pretty, dark-haired woman approached our table.

"Thank you for watching Shelby."

"You can pay me back in the future," Sebastian said.

The woman snorted and laughed. "You'd have to settle down first."

"I didn't necessarily mean children. There are other things you can do to return the favor."

"Like deliver your car to you, so you don't have to Uber back to it?" she said with a grin. She turned to me, holding out her hand. "Hi, I'm Angela, Sebastian's big sister. I hope Shelby wasn't too much trouble."

I stood and shook her hand. "Hello. I'm Pru. And, no, Shelby was great."

"I still appreciate you letting her come along for the food tasting."

Sebastian cut in. "I tried to give her a bunch of sugar, so she'd run circles around you when she got home, but it backfired, and she crashed instead."

"You did not," Angela said.

I smiled at the dynamic between the siblings.

"Did you really bring Sebastian's car?" I asked, hoping that we wouldn't have to wait for an Uber to leave.

Angela smiled. "I did."

"How?"

"I have a spare key, and my husband and I met at home. We took his vehicle to pick up Sebastian's car to bring here."

"That was nice of you."

"You still owe me," Sebastian said.

I smacked him on the arm. "You're mean."

Angela rolled her eyes. "I'm used to it." Picking up Shelby's pink backpack, she said, "Okay, kiddo, are you ready to go home?" she asked even though Shelby was still asleep. She picked her daughter up and placed her head on her shoulder.

"Do you need help?" Sebastian asked.

Maybe he isn't that mean.

"No, I've got it. Luis is waiting for me outside." She glanced at me. "Nice to meet you."

"You too."

"Thanks for bringing my car," Sebastian said as Angela walked away.

"You're welcome," she called over her shoulder.

I looked at Sebastian. "Can you give me a ride back to my car?"

"Sure, but it'll cost you."

Chapter Twenty-One

SEBASTIAN

PRU SHIFTED in the passenger seat toward me. "So, what is this ride going to cost me?"

My brow furrowed. "Huh?"

"Back at the restaurant, you said this ride was going to cost me."

I smiled. "I guess I did." After paying for the extra food I had ordered for Shelby before we could leave, I had forgotten I had said that just to tease her.

Pru moved closer. "So, what were you thinking?"

Right now, I was thinking about the glint in her eye and the way her shirt was pulling against her breasts.

"About what?" I asked.

She laughed. "About the payment for the ride."

"Oh. You know I was joking, right? I'm the reason you don't have your car."

"That's too bad. I was thinking a blow job."

Stunned into silence, I could only stare out the windshield.

"I mean, I would never blackmail sexual favors for rides from anyone, but I wouldn't turn that down if someone wanted to give me one as a thank-you."

"Hmm, interesting that you say someone and not women."

I grinned at her. "I'm an equal opportunity recipient. I would never limit the magnificence of my cock to just women."

Pru sighed and closed her eyes in exasperation.

I put my hand on her knee and squeezed. "I'm kidding, Pru."

"About which part?" she asked after she opened her eyes.

Her face was serious, even after I'd told her I was joking.

"The part about how great my dick is. I know that half the population has them and that they aren't as special as we penis owners think they are."

Pru moved the shoulder strap part of her seat belt behind her and leaned forward, rubbing her hand over my crotch. "So, you'd be okay with a man giving you head?"

I shrugged. "Sure."

She half-gasped, half-laughed. "No way."

"Would it feel good? Yes. Why would I say no?"

"Because some men can't stand the thought of another guy doing anything remotely sexual with them."

"I'll be honest. It doesn't turn me on like it does when I

picture you, but I'm not repulsed by it, and I don't understand those who are."

Pru unzipped my jeans. "Are you saying you've pictured me going down on you?" she asked, tugging my underwear down and pulling my very hard cock out of my pants.

"Fuck." I sucked in a breath and forced myself to keep my eyes on the road. When she'd first touched me, I'd thought she was teasing me back. But now, I was worried I was going to put us into a ditch.

Her fist wrapped around my length, and she stroked me.

I stopped her with my hand on her wrist. "This is the type of thing that causes accidents. It's the ones where we firefighters and paramedics laugh when we hear how it was caused."

Carefully, she pulled my arm away, and I let her.

"That's why you have to concentrate. Now, Sebastian?"

I glanced her way.

"You didn't answer my question. Have you pictured me going down on you?"

"I'm a guy. I'd be lying if I said I hadn't."

"Hmm. Good answer." She pushed up my center console, leaned all the way over, and drew me into her mouth.

"Holy shit," I muttered as I almost swerved into the next lane. "Pru, I don't think you should be doing th—" The last word sounded like I was choking on something because that was when she decided to lick the crown of my dick.

Her hot, wet mouth felt amazing, and when she sucked me to the back of her throat, I knew my attention on the road was fading. And with Pru barely in a seat belt anymore, I had to either get her to stop—even though I wanted to die like this someday—or I needed to get to the lot where her car was parked.

Thankfully, we were close, but not quite close enough. I needed to get her attention on something else long enough for me to park my own car.

"Pru."

"Hmm?" she hummed around my dick.

That didn't help.

"Are you wet? I want you to put your hand in your panties and tell me if you're wet."

She propped her right foot on the passenger seat and slid her hand into her pants. She pulled her head up and back against my stomach, panting.

"Are you wet?"

She nodded.

"Push your fingers inside your pussy. Get them real wet for me and then give me your hand."

She whimpered a few seconds later but did as I'd commanded.

As soon as her arm was close, I snatched her hand and pushed her fingers into my mouth.

I'd only gone down on her once, but I already recognized the unique flavor that was Pru Maxwell. "Fuck, you taste good."

We passed under a streetlight, and I managed to catch the dreamy, satisfied smile on her face.

"Do you have a condom in your purse?" I asked.

She nodded again.

"Good. We'll be to your car in just a few minutes. I need you to find that condom for me as soon as we get there."

Taking the hand that had just been in my mouth, she wrapped it around my cock and sucked on the tip. "If you plan to fuck me in your car, it's not going to be easy."

I laughed. "This isn't my first rodeo, baby."

In what felt like forever but was really only about another thirty seconds, I was pulling into the parking lot. Thankfully, the catering business was not a restaurant, so there were only a few cars parked outside, and it was absent of people.

Still, I found a spot in the corner under a tree and put my car in park.

Pru sat up, and I unbuckled my seat belt. I pulled up my pants just enough so that if someone was out there and saw me, they wouldn't see all of me, and I exited the driver's side while she rummaged through her bag.

I strode over to the passenger side and opened the door. Reaching between Pru's legs, I pulled the lever under the seat and repositioned it all the way back.

"Do you have that condom?" I asked, my face inches away from hers.

She held up the rubber between her first two fingers.

I brushed my lips over hers. "Good girl," I said and took it from her.

Standing, I unwrapped the condom, and with the smoothness of someone who'd been protecting himself since he'd lost his virginity, I pulled out my dick and slid that fucker on.

With Pru's help, I lifted her just enough so that I could slide underneath her and shut the door. Together, we pushed down her pants past her knees.

"You ready?"

Taking my hand and placing it between her legs, she told me, "Yes."

She wasn't lying. She was soaked for me.

I raised her ass up and placed my cock at her entrance. Then, I slowly lowered her back down until she was sitting on my lap with me fully inside her. I bit her shoulder. "Fuck, you feel incredible."

She reached behind me and grabbed the back of my neck. "So do you."

"I hate to do this, but we're sitting in a parking lot, half-naked. We'd better make it quick."

"As long as you make it good, I can do quick."

"That sounds like a challenge."

"Make of it what you will," she said as I started rocking her hips over me. "Mmm...yeah, just like that."

Despite that I'd pointed out we were in a rush, neither of us seemed to be in a hurry in the beginning.

I pushed her braids off of one shoulder and kissed the

back of her neck, simply enjoying the feel of our bodies being connected.

But even with my eyes closed, I sensed the brightness of headlights passing by us.

"Ooh," Pru said and lifted her arm.

Dammit, whoever was out there was going to ruin a good thing.

Fumbling around the side of the seat, I found the lever and pulled. I forced the back to recline all the way.

With the new position, I was able to fuck her from below. I felt like a man on a mission as I drove in and out of her. As I thrust, I ran one hand over her breast, pinching her nipple and rolling it between my fingers. My other hand was firmly on her clit. I wanted to make sure this woman came when I did.

"Tell me when you're close," I told her.

A few seconds later, she clamped her legs closed over my fingers and ground her ass into my pelvis as she exploded. My fingers were soaked within seconds as her pussy clenched around my cock.

"Fuck," I said, letting myself ride the climax wave. Knowing I had that effect on her body only made it that much stronger.

With my arm wrapped around Pru's waist, I held her as we lay there, panting. I was still inside her, and I could feel gentle pulses from her pussy every few seconds. I was pretty confident I had made her orgasm very good if I was feeling aftershocks.

Her head was next to mine, half on my shoulder, half

on the seat, when she turned her head and kissed my jaw. "That was amazing…"

I chuckled. "But?"

She nuzzled me with her nose. "But I regret that I didn't get to taste you."

My cock jumped at the thought.

I kissed her forehead. "Next time."

Her body stiffened ever so slightly—it was so subtle that I almost missed it—but just as quickly, she relaxed.

I arched my head back, so I could study her face. "Are you hurt?"

She smiled as if my question was absurd. "Not in the slightest."

This was good news. Especially since I didn't want our night to end.

I ran my hand over her cheek. "Come over tonight."

She didn't say anything.

"Or I can come to your place?" I smiled. "I haven't been there yet."

"Uh, yeah." Pru opened the door, got off my lap, and stood before I even knew what was going on.

I watched her button and zip up her pants that she had somehow yanked up while getting out of the car with me sitting underneath her.

Feeling exposed, I pulled up my own pants and removed the condom before throwing it in the plastic bag I kept in my vehicle for trash.

"Can you hand me my purse?" she asked.

"I guess this means the night is done?"

"I think it's for the best."

I scoffed and swung my legs out onto the ground. I made sure to grab her bag when I stood.

"Here," I said, pushing it to her chest.

"Are you mad?"

I stepped out of the way and closed the passenger door. "Nah. I don't waste time getting mad at women for not wanting to be with me."

"Because you'll just find someone else instead."

I raised my brow. "You said it. Not me."

Of course I wasn't going to find someone else tonight. I'd just had a great orgasm after an evening of eating. I was going home and going to bed.

Would it have been more fun to spend more time with Pru? Sure. Was I going to cry because she didn't want to spend more time with me? No.

"I can't believe you." She actually sounded mad at me.

I had to laugh, which only made her more upset.

I stepped forward and yanked her toward me. Bending down, I kissed her long and thoroughly. "You have a good night." I slapped her butt. "We'll talk again soon."

With that, I spun on my heel, got in my car, and left.

Chapter Twenty-Two

PRU

"I DON'T SEE anything I like," Elizabeth said, moving hangers across the clothing rack.

It was Saturday afternoon, and I was helping her shop for work clothes. Elizabeth didn't like dressing up, but it was required for her job, so about twice a year, I took it upon myself to be her personal stylist.

"Me neither," I said. "I used to love this store, but they don't have the selections they used to have."

Elizabeth shoved a hanger to one side till it smacked into another and gasped. "You don't think this means we're getting old, do you?"

"Nope." I adamantly shook my head. "I refuse. We are still young."

"I agree. But can we go somewhere where the shorts are long enough to cover my vagina?"

"Absolutely."

As we headed out of the store in the mall, we both

turned right. Elizabeth hated clothes shopping, so we always hit the same stores in the same order; however, I feared we might need to add a few new places to the list of shopping possibilities.

"So, how did things go with Isabelle?" I asked. I hadn't brought it up yet, hoping that maybe she would want to talk to me first, but I'd been dying to know what had happened since the weekend before.

Elizabeth shrugged. "I don't know." She seemed wistful.

"What don't you know? Did the two of you go on your date?"

"Yes, but it felt like any other time we hang out."

"Oh." That hadn't occurred to me. I'd thought things would be great with them from the beginning. "So, nothing physical happened then?"

Elizabeth sighed. "No. Not that I had expected a lot, but I'd thought we'd maybe hold hands. Maybe a kiss."

I put my arm around her. "I'm sorry." I dropped my hand and asked, "Did she turn you down?"

"No."

"Then, I don't understand."

She looked away, embarrassed. "I never even tried."

"Elizabeth." I hip-checked her with a laugh. "No wonder nothing happened."

"I know. I guess I thought since I had bid on her, she would make the first move."

I winced. "That's tough. I mean, Isabelle has never dated a woman before. She's probably not going to make the first move. What did she say when you talked about the auction and why you bid on her?"

Elizabeth laughed nervously. "We didn't talk about it."

I stopped and shook my head. "I'm done with you."

She laughed and grabbed my hand. "Don't leave me. I ripped my favorite black pants, and I need a replacement."

"Fine," I said, pretending sticking around was a hardship. "I guess I can stay and still help you."

"Thank you."

"All joking aside, you know that you need to talk to Isabelle. She's probably more confused than you are."

Elizabeth sucked in a big breath.

"Breathe," I reminded her.

She exhaled. "I know. I'm so nervous. I've had a crush on her for so long. What if she doesn't see me that way?"

That was a difficult question. It was one thing to like someone who didn't like you back, knowing in the back of your head that things changed, people grew, and tastes evolved. But when you liked someone who wasn't attracted to your gender, then that was it. And Isabelle had only dated men.

"If she doesn't see you like that, then you will cry for a day or two, and then you will move on. Your friendship might suffer a bit, but I have every confidence you two won't let something like that break it up for good. And once you know for sure there is no chance, you will start to move on. And you will find a woman who loves you for you." I grinned. "And you'll find a woman who wants to get naked and have sex with you too."

Elizabeth smiled. "Thanks for making me feel better."

"That's what friends are for." I tilted my head to the side. "Shall we keep walking?"

"Yes, but speaking of sex, how did it go with Sebastian the other night?"

"Ugh," I said and took off for our next destination. "I don't want to talk about it," I said when Elizabeth caught up to me.

"A dud in bed, huh?"

I laughed at the thought of Sebastian hearing that. He would be so offended.

"No. Unfortunately, he's the exact opposite. I wish he were bad in bed though."

That would have made my life easier. Because I wouldn't be regretting my decision today. Instead, I wished I had gone home with him last night. One quickie orgasm in a car like we were in high school had not been enough.

"I'm officially confused."

"The sex was great." I raised my hands. "Magnificent. Dare I say, the best I've ever—" I shook my head. "Nope. I'm not going to say it."

Elizabeth was staring at me, eyebrows raised.

"Anyway, we had great sex a few times, and then in the morning, I went home. That should have been the end of it."

"But?"

"But then he had to get all possessive in a text."

"Doesn't that turn you on?"

I clenched my hands together. "*Yes.*" I threw them

open. "But no. I don't want someone trying to control me and who I talk to." I explained to her about asking for Rory's phone number and Sebastian telling me no and that no men would be fucking me while he was fucking me.

"Damn, he went there, didn't he?"

"He did."

"What did you say after that?"

"I corrected him. I pointed out he *had* fucked me. Past tense."

"What did he say?"

" 'We'll see about that.' " At this point, it was kind of our comeback to each other.

"The guy has an ego on him."

"Yes." I sighed. "But then he does something really sweet, like take care of his three-year-old niece during our tastings."

"He did what now?"

I told Elizabeth about how Sebastian had shown up at the food tasting because he had found out about it and how Rory had been sick. And then how Sebastian had volunteered to babysit his niece.

"It was really cute to watch them together."

"It sounds like last night was good. Are you still conflicted?"

"Yes, because we had sex. In his car."

"Wow. Was it even good?"

"Yes. That man could make sex good literally anyplace. But when we were done, he said something about next time and asked me to come over."

Elizabeth scratched her head. "You lost me. Why is that bad? I get the possessive texts didn't sit well with you, but was that the only one? And it sounds like you had fun last night."

"It's not bad. It's just..."

She took my arm and pulled me close as we walked. "I understand that we started our little club because we were sick of men—or in my case, secretly unattracted to them—but we all knew deep down that it was just for fun. None of you were really swearing off men for the rest of your lives. At least, that's what I thought."

"I don't know what I want. I love the freedom of being single, I like having my bed to myself, and you know how strong-willed I am."

Elizabeth mock gasped. "You don't say."

"You're funny."

"I know," she said with a grin.

"But I admit, seeing our friends happy and in love does make me envious. And they really did get some good guys. But the thing is, I'm so damn picky and not rational. I don't want some pushover guy. It does nothing for me. Sorry to all the beta men out there; you are gems, but you don't trip my trigger. But strong men like Sebastian...well, they can get too controlling."

"Yikes."

"That's maybe not the right description for all of them because I like to be in control too. They like to be too involved. I want to do what I want, when I want, and I don't want to answer to anyone."

Elizabeth wrinkled her nose. "But if this guy was doing things and going places, wouldn't you want to know where he was? Reasonably speaking."

"Yes," I admitted. "I warned you, I'm picky."

"I think you might be lumping all guys together and you need to give some of them a chance as individuals."

I looked away. "Well, that's where my other problem comes into play."

"What's that?"

"He'll want to spend all this time with me, wooing me over with his dick, and then when he's done with me, he'll be done. Meanwhile, I will have let my guard down and actually want something more serious."

When Elizabeth didn't say anything, I turned to see if I could read her expression.

"What?" I asked at the look of pure speculation on her face.

"So, last night, you didn't want to go to his house because you want to keep it casual, but now, you're saying you'll fall in love and he'll dump you? Are you the non-serious partner or the serious one in the situation?"

"I told you, I'm not being rational."

"I'll say."

I laughed again. "Not helping."

"Okay." She squeezed my arm. "I think you are one hundred percent a control freak. You are trying to control the tenth step of this relationship when the two of you are on step two. You need to loosen up a little and just see where things go. You are coming up with scenarios that haven't even happened yet or even *will* happen."

"I know; I know. You're right."

"When will you see him again?"

"I'm not sure. I'm almost done planning his fundraiser."

"But you're not finished yet. Nothing like having a good excuse to see someone," Elizabeth pointed out.

"You're right about that. When are you going to see Isabelle?"

"I'm not sure exactly, but soon."

"You and I are quite the pair, aren't we?" I said.

"Yes, we are."

"Good thing we're almost to the next store. We need to get out of our own heads."

"And find me some black pants."

As we walked into the store, I knew I felt better. I didn't know why I was getting so worked up about a man I'd sworn I didn't even like in the first place. I needed to let things happen as they came. And it was nice I had an excuse to see him this coming week, but after that, I didn't know what would happen. We were almost done planning, and the fundraiser was going to come and go before I knew it. Then, there was a chance I wouldn't see Sebastian again at all.

Chapter Twenty-Three

SEBASTIAN

I WAS JUST JUMPING out of the fire truck on Monday when my phone buzzed in my pocket. We'd come from a cardiac arrest that most of us hadn't been able to shake off. We were often the first on the scene, including today. But even with our EMT training and the paramedics showing up minutes after us, we'd watched a man who wasn't quite fifty pass away in front of his wife and two kids. And it wasn't even ten yet.

I didn't really want to speak to anyone at the moment, but incidents like today showed me that life was short, and I never knew who could be on the other side, trying to get ahold of me.

I wasn't expecting it to be Pru. I wasn't exactly happy about it either.

Pru: Good morning.

I hadn't heard from Pru all weekend, and I was irritated that she'd chosen to contact me today.

> Me: Morning.

> Pru: I have one thing left on my list for us to take care of.

> Me: What's that?

I had thought we were done. We had location, food, and Pru was taking care of the decorations. But it figured she was only texting me about the fundraiser.

> Pru: DJ. I have a few choices, and I have information to help you decide on who you'd like to hire, so I'd like you to come to my office today, if possible.

> Me: I'm at work.

> Pru: Evening is fine. I can wait. How about after six? How does that sound?

She must really want to get rid of me.

I was tempted to tell her to just pick a DJ herself, but I had learned my lesson from last time. I might as well get it over with.

> Me: That works.

> Pru: See you then.

Me: See you then.

I turned off my screen in case she texted me anything else. I really wasn't in the mood to see her tonight. If she fucked me in her office and kicked me out after, I wasn't sure what I would do. And I didn't want to find out.

I headed toward the locker room and saw Rory walk down the hall.

"Hey," I called out to him.

He spun around and pointed to himself. "Me?"

"Yeah."

Rory jogged over.

He had been so disappointed about missing the food tasting, but I was pretty sure I had something that was going to cheer him up. Unlike me, who wanted to go home and be alone tonight, Rory always wanted to be around people.

"Pru has one more thing for me to do before we're done with the fundraising planning. How would you feel about picking out the DJ for the event?"

Rory's eyes lit up. "You're joking."

He was so happy that I couldn't help but smile.

"I'm serious. She wants to do it tonight, but I can't make it. You want to fill in for me?"

"You're going to let me do it all by myself?"

I laughed. "I mean, Pru will be there to help, but yes." I slapped him on the back. "I trust you."

"Wow."

"Does this mean you're saying yes?" I mentally crossed my fingers.

"Hell yes. I love music."

"Ooh. A *hell yes*. Rory means business."

"Are you sure you don't want to come?"

With Rory there, it would be easier to avoid getting naked with Pru, but once Rory left, there was no guarantee. I didn't need another night of hot sex, followed by rejection. Most of the time, Pru's *hot and cold* routine was cute, but I was too raw today.

"Yeah, I'm sure. Send my regards to her."

"I will." He pulled out his phone. "Should I tell her I'm coming?"

I put my hand on his cell and pushed it down. "No. Let's make it a surprise."

I wasn't asking Rory to go, so then she could text me five minutes from now and ask me why I wasn't.

"I like surprises."

It was a good thing he did because I had a feeling Pru hated them.

———

PRU

Six o'clock sharp, there was a knock at my office door.

I stood and smoothed down my black skirt. I had picked it out because it showed off my ass and hugged my hips. I was hoping Sebastian wouldn't be able to keep his hands off me when he saw it.

It had been three days since we'd had sex, and I was really regretting not going home with him on Friday.

"Come in," I said.

The door opened a smidgen, and Rory stuck his head in.

"Hi, Pru," he said, grin plastered on his face.

What the fuck is Rory doing here?

"Hi, Rory. You can come in." I motioned him inside.

"Thanks," he said, pushing the door open all the way.

My eyes were glued to that hallway behind him. "Where's Sebastian?"

"He couldn't make it tonight, so he sent me instead." Rory held out his arms. "Surprise."

I groaned under my breath. I hated surprises.

"Come in and sit down," I said, hoping he couldn't see the mixture of disappointment and annoyance on my face.

"Thanks." He looked around. "You have a nice office."

"Thank you." I pulled out the folders I had with the information about the DJs and cleared my throat. "When I messaged Sebastian earlier today, he said he was coming. Do you know what happened?"

"No. He had some other plans and couldn't make it."

"Here is the information for you to look at," I told Rory as I sat back in my chair.

Sebastian hadn't mentioned any plans when I talked to him. Had he lied to me, or had he made plans after we

155

finished texting? And I hated the little voice in my head that was asking if it was with another woman.

More than that, I really hated that I cared. This was exactly what I'd told Elizabeth I was worried about. And I hadn't even seen him again.

I knew I was better off being alone.

Chapter Twenty-Four

SEBASTIAN

FRIDAY, I was going through inventory at work when my captain approached me.

"Creed."

I stiffened at the sound of his voice and slowly turned. "Captain," I said with a nod.

"How's the fundraiser planning going?" He smirked. "We are running out of time. Announcements need to be made soon."

The asshole was taking glee in the fact that he thought I was going to mess up.

"And what if I'm not ready in time?"

"Gosh." He rubbed his chin. "We'll have to tell everyone you couldn't quite do it. But maybe they'll understand. Maybe you could explain to them that making lieutenant was too much for you and you weren't ready for so much responsibility."

Yeah, I bet this asshole would like that.

"Thank God then," I said, half-serious, half-mocking.

Captain frowned. "What? Why *thank God*?"

"Because I got all the information into the business office earlier this week. I'm surprised you didn't already get your invitation."

The fundraiser had been on the city calendar since last year's event, but now, with the location reserved, the actual invitations could go out.

With the big event looming closer and specifics needing to be finalized soon, I had no doubt the captain had chosen today to speak to me. He hadn't checked in once before this, nor offered me any help.

What a dick.

"I don't believe you."

"I suppose it would be beneficial to us both if you did, but you don't have to. You are more than welcome to call..." I bit my lip, as if I were trying to recall a name. I snapped my fingers. "Ruth. You can call Ruth at the business office. She said that I had done a good job and was very excited to attend the fundraiser."

"You really have everything done?"

"Yep. Last thing on the list was the DJ, and that was taken care of earlier this week."

Rory had been very excited when he told me about his meeting with Pru, and I was glad I had sent him. I regretted not getting a chance to see her now that I was in a better mood, but it was worth it to make Rory's day.

"Is there anything else, Captain?"

His reply was interrupted by the alarm going off and the announcement of a pileup on the interstate.

Saved by the bell.

PRU

"I'm on my way," I said, trying to keep my tone even.

The client I was working with was one of those difficult ones. I had done everything she'd asked for and then some, and she always demanded more. And was she ever grateful? No. Had she said *thank you* even once? No. She was making it hard for me to work with her, and I couldn't wait to be done.

"I'll be waiting," she snapped.

The client had literally asked me fifteen minutes ago to meet with her last minute, and now, she was upset I couldn't get there any faster.

I ended my phone call by smashing my finger on my car's console and screamed out some obscenities. I didn't want to talk to her again because I needed to calm down, so I turned off my phone and threw it on the passenger seat.

My mood had already been crappy because I hadn't heard from Sebastian all week.

I had texted him after the meeting with Rory last week to ask him if everything was okay. He had responded with a single *all good*, and that was it. I refused to message him again, but it seemed like he felt the same. At this point, I didn't know who was avoiding who anymore.

Gripping the steering wheel, I took a couple of deep breaths. In for ten seconds and out for ten seconds.

My irritation began to lower, and I was feeling calmer, to the point that I realized what time it was.

Shit. I was supposed to call my boss almost ten minutes ago, but I had been distracted.

I was about to reach for my cell when the vehicle in front of me hit their brakes. I quickly did the same and managed to slow down while they sped up before I got too close to them, but my cell went flying off the seat. And because it was turned off, I couldn't use my car's Bluetooth until I turned it back on.

Today was not my day.

The good news was, I could see my phone, and all I had to do was reach over and pick it up. Thankfully, it hadn't ended up hiding in the corner. The bad news was, I was still on the interstate, and taking the time to get off so I could stop would only make me later to meet my difficult client.

I waited until I had about five car lengths between the vehicle in front of me and mine, and I quickly leaned down to snatch my cell from the floormat. I missed the first time, but the second time was a success.

"Ha-ha," I said as I jerked back up.

But my happiness turned to fright as all the vehicles in front of me were stopped. It looked like there was an accident up ahead, but that was all I caught before I slammed on my brakes and winced.

Next thing I knew, there was a loud crunch of metal on metal, a pain worse than any hangover in my head, and blackness.

———

"Ma'am, ma'am. Are you okay?"

I opened my eyes, and when the pain from the bright lights hit my pupils, making the agony in my head worse, I immediately closed them.

"Ma'am?"

I groaned.

"I think she's awake," the same voice yelled but from farther away.

All I knew was, it sounded like a woman.

"What's going on?" I mumbled.

"You were in a car accident."

My eyes flipped open again. Immediately, I squinted as I adjusted to the light. The light that was bothering me was the sun, and as my memory returned, I remembered my phone falling, me picking it up, and my foot hitting the brakes too late.

I tried to look over at the clock in my car, but the air bag was in the way, and my seat belt wouldn't budge.

"Ma'am, I don't think you should be moving. You could have a neck injury."

Despite her warning, I turned my head to see the woman who had been speaking to me. I didn't remember putting my window down, and it took me a moment to realize it was because all the glass had broken out of it. The woman looked to be a few years younger than me and scared out of her mind.

"I didn't hit you, did I?"

"Oh, no. I stopped when I saw you hit the semi in front of you."

"I hit a semi?"

"Yes."

"That explains it."

"Explains what?"

"Why I feel like I've been hit by a truck."

The woman laughed but only for a second before her eyes widened and she slammed a hand over her mouth.

"I'm Pru," I told her.

"Pru, I'm Faith." She reached into my car and picked up my hand. "I called 911 before I even stopped, so someone should be here soon. I'll stay with you until they get here."

"Thank you." I licked my lips and realized how dry my mouth felt. "Can you tell me what time it is?"

Faith used her free hand to look at her phone and answered my question.

I started laughing until it hurt my side too much.

"What's so funny?"

"I'm super late to meet a client from hell. But when I tell her what happened, she can't even be mad at me." My smile fell as a realization came to me. "Never mind. She's the type of person who will still be mad."

Faith smiled. "I've dealt with people like that before. They're the worst."

I caught the sound of sirens now, and they gradually got louder.

"I bet you'll be out of here in no time. A fire truck is pulling up," Faith told me, smile on her face.

Somehow, I found the strength to pull her closer. "What city are we in?"

She looked around. "I don't know."

I wasn't surprised. Driving through the metro area, you could go through multiple towns to get from point A to point B.

"What does the truck say?" I asked.

"I don't—"

I squeezed her hand, and she lifted her other to shield the sun.

"The side says *Golden Prairie Fire Department*."

I had been afraid of that. But Sebastian hadn't worked last Friday. Maybe he wasn't working today either.

I listened as someone started barking out orders, and when I heard, "Creed and Nelson, you're on the Lexus," I let go of Faith's hand.

"Fuck me."

Chapter Twenty-Five

SEBASTIAN

WHEN I SAW the black Lexus, I immediately thought of Pru, but I figured that was because she'd been on my mind with all the talk of the fundraiser.

I pushed her to the back of my mind. I needed to focus on my job. Dispatch had called us to this accident, and while we were on our way, a second car accident had occurred. It was something I had seen before on the interstate. Due to their high driving speed, people weren't always prepared for the traffic jams that seemed to come out of nowhere.

There was a woman standing outside of the Lexus, who I addressed first as we were approaching.

"Are you injured?" I called out to her.

She shook her head. "Oh, no. I wasn't in the accident. I only stopped to help."

"How many people are in the car?"

"One woman."

"Conscious?" I asked as the bystander moved out of the way.

"I'm awake," a familiar voice said as Nelson and I reached the car.

My stomach dropped at the sound of Pru's voice, but I didn't want her to know I was scared.

I grinned and rested my arms on top of the car. "Prudence Maxwell. If you wanted to see me again, you could have done it in a much easier way."

"Ha-ha," she said.

"You two know each other?" Nelson asked.

"Yes," I said.

"I'm the one helping Sebastian plan your fundraiser," Pru told him.

"My condolences," Nelson told her. "Working with Sebastian is almost as bad as getting in a car accident."

I knew Nelson was getting Pru to relax, so I didn't take offense to his joke.

Pru liked it though because she started laughing, but then she immediately stopped. "*Ow.*" She grabbed her side. "That fricking hurt."

My smile dropped, and I straightened. "Don't worry, Pru; we'll get you out of there as soon as possible."

———

I paced inside Pru's ER room while I waited for her to return from radiology. It wasn't really a room, but an area closed off by a curtain.

After the scenes of both accidents had been cleared, I'd asked my captain if I could leave work early to go and see Pru. I'd thought for sure after the conversation we'd had earlier today, he would have taken immense satisfaction in telling me no, but he had let me go. And he had found someone to cover my weekend shift too. Maybe the guy wasn't a complete asshole.

Unfortunately, by the time I had gotten there from work, Pru had already left to get X-rays and CTs, so I hadn't seen her since Nelson and I had freed her from her car and the paramedics hauled her off to the hospital. I was starting to get anxious, but I knew I wouldn't be able to get any information about her due to privacy laws. I was lucky they'd even shown me where her room was.

Finally, after what felt like forever, Pru came back. As she was being wheeled in headfirst by the radiology tech, a nurse came in behind her.

"Thanks, Judy. I can hook the patient back up," the nurse whose name tag read *Shawn* said to the tech. Then, he looked at me and Pru. "Did you see you have a guest?" he said to her.

Pru turned her head in my direction. "What are you doing here?"

Shawn raised his eyebrows. "You want me to kick him out?" The look on his face said he would absolutely do that if Pru said yes.

"No," Pru said with a sigh. "He can stay."

Shawn turned to his patient's IV and then started doing something on the computer.

Pru looked at me again. "But what are you doing here?" She scanned me up and down, eyeing my street clothes. "Shouldn't you be at work?"

"I told my captain my girlfriend was one of the people in the car accident and he let me leave early. He even gave me the weekend off."

Pru scowled. "I'm not your girlfriend."

I snorted. "Don't I know it?"

Somehow, her scowl worsened.

I pulled up the folding chair that was in the corner, sat down, and took her hand. "What did the doctor say? I noticed they took your C collar off."

"Yeah, they took it off after my CT, but I don't know the rest of my results yet. I feel like one big bruise."

Shawn looked at Pru with sympathy just as the doctor walked in.

Pru pulled her hand from mine.

"Good news, Pru," the doctor said. "Nothing is broken, so you probably bruised your ribs. And no head bleeds, so that leaves you with a nice concussion." She smiled. "Overall, not the best news, but it could be worse."

"What does this mean for me?" Pru asked.

"You're going to have to take it easy for some weeks, maybe months, while your ribs heal. Your concussion will heal faster, but we'd like you to stay overnight in case things get worse."

Pru groaned. "Please, I just want to go home. I promise I won't do anything but rest. Even if I want to do anything more than walk to the bathroom, I won't."

The doctor's eyes darted to me and back to Pru. "If you have someone who can take you home and stay with you for at least twenty-four hours, I might consider letting you leave."

I waited to see if Pru would ask me to stay with her. She glanced my way but didn't say a word.

Stubborn woman.

"I'll stay with her. And if I told you I was a licensed EMT, would that convince you to let her go home?"

"I don't want you to do that," Pru said in a low voice to me.

I chuckled. "Too bad. I'm taking care of you whether you want me to or not."

She tried to glare at me, but I figured the idea of getting out of the hospital made it too hard for her to fully commit.

Out of the corner of my eye, the doctor looked at the nurse.

"Oh, he's not actually her boyfriend, but he left work early and took off the whole weekend to take care of our patient. I think she's in good hands."

Pru crossed her arms over her chest and winced for a split second. "No, thank you. I'll stay here tonight."

The doctor looked like she was biting the inside of her cheek, so she wouldn't laugh. She cleared her throat and schooled her face. "I'm going to wait until everything is back—we're still waiting on some labs—and then I'll release you into the care of this gentleman right here."

"But I said I'd rather stay here," Pru said.

"If I had to stay in a hospital room with one nurse who

had several other patients or receive one-on-one care from an EMT at *home*, I would pick the latter," Shawn said.

"It's the one-on-one care I'm worried about," Pru muttered.

I looked down at the floor to hide my laugh. When I lifted my head, I took Pru's hand and squeezed. "Don't worry, babe. I won't give you the Sebastian special until you're well enough to really enjoy it."

The doctor and Nurse Shawn laughed, but Pru yanked her hand from mine with a sound of disgust and rolled her eyes.

Chapter Twenty-Six

PRU

"ONE MORE STEP."

"I *know*," I said, snapping at Sebastian. "I've lived here for six years."

He raised his brow but didn't say a word.

"I'm sorry," I muttered once we were through the front door. "I'm just..."

"Someone who has been in a car accident. It's okay to be frustrated, Pru." He led me to the living room. "Couch or recliner? Or bed?"

"Recliner."

I was afraid that if I lay on the couch, I wouldn't be able to get up. And it was still early evening. I wasn't ready to go to bed yet even if I was tired. I refused to let the accident take any more from me. I'd already lost my car; I was out of work for at least a week, the doctor had said; and I couldn't even drive myself around.

Sebastian helped me sit with a groan. Even with pain meds, my side still ached.

He crouched down on his heels. "Listen, I know you like being in control and not at someone's mercy, but you can trust me, okay?"

I didn't like being called out like that even if he was right.

But before I could tell him to shove off, he stood. "Now that we had that talk, where are your clean clothes?"

I couldn't tell him I was mad now because I really wanted clean clothes. I'd had to put on the torn, dirty work clothes I'd had on during the accident.

Maybe it was best I pretended like his comment had had no effect on me.

I smiled politely, trying to infuse nonchalance into my body. "The tall dresser, middle drawer. I should have clean pajamas in there."

"Bedroom?"

Funny. We'd had sex twice, and I'd spent the night at his house, but this was the first time he'd been to my house.

I gave him directions and pulled my phone out of my purse.

While I was still at the hospital, a police officer had brought my stuff to me, and surprisingly, the item that had caused the accident had survived in one piece.

I pulled up my text messages. The first thing I saw was several from the client I'd been on the way to see. There were some hostile messages, including one where she called me a bitch. Then, there were two more that must have come in after my boss had contacted her about the accident, telling me she was sorry we couldn't meet up and that she hoped I was okay. Oh, and could I still plan her event?

I sent my boss a quick message, letting her know I'd be out of work for a while. Cherry could tell the asshole client I wasn't working for her anymore because I was done.

Next, I pulled up the group thread with my man-hater club friends and sighed.

I didn't want to *not* tell them, but I didn't want to tell them either. I wanted some peace and quiet tonight. However, I knew that if one of them had been in an accident, I would want to know.

> Me: Hello, my beautiful friends. I was in a car accident this afternoon. I'm okay—a little bruised and banged up, but I am home. I'm really tired and headed to bed soon. I know you all will have questions, and I will be happy to answer them tomorrow. Love you all!

I hit Send, turned off my screen, and closed my eyes.

I heard Sebastian enter the living room just as my phone rang, but before I could even check the caller ID, it was swiped from my lap.

"Hey," Sebastian said. "Yes, I'm here with Pru." He held up my pajamas with a questioning look on his face, so I nodded. "No, she's not dying, and no, you can't talk to her. Pru needs to relax and get some rest, so she can heal. No phone calls. Spread the word."

He hit End and set my cell on the end table.

I stared at him, mouth open. He'd just told off someone. If I wasn't injured, I would think it was sexy.

"Who was that?"

"Bree."

"Wow, that was kind of rude."

He knelt on the floor and set my PJs on the arm of my recliner. "You don't need anyone bothering you. She won't take it personally."

He was right.

"Shirt or pants first?" he asked.

"Huh?"

"Do you want to change your shirt or pants first?"

"Shirt, I guess," I answered, not sure why he'd asked.

Sebastian grabbed my hips and gently pulled me toward him, and then he reached for my shirt.

I was about to tell him I could do it myself, but the second I tried to help, I felt a sharp pain.

"Hey, slow down. There's no rush," he said in a soothing tone.

I relaxed and let him do his thing. But I hated feeling like a helpless child. At the hospital, a female nurse had come in to help me get dressed, which had seemed okay at the time. It was different with Sebastian.

When my shirt was off, he looked at me with fake shock. "Wow, this is the first time I've ever undressed a woman."

"Shut up," I said with a laugh.

He smiled and put my clean shirt over my head. Then,

he reached behind me and unclasped my bra before putting my arms in my sleeves. He purposely pulled the shirt down to my waist before taking off my bra through the shirtsleeve. That had to be something he'd learned from a woman.

"You've done this before," I said with amazement.

"Done what?" he said.

"Helped a woman get dressed."

He looked up at me. "You know, I have been in relationships before." When I blinked at him, he said, "Serious ones." He leaned in and whispered, "I even lived with a girlfriend for three years."

I didn't know why I was so surprised. It wasn't like Sebastian had ever said he was afraid of commitment or that he wouldn't get serious with a woman. That was something I had subconsciously assumed all on my own.

As Sebastian reached for the waistband of my pants and slowly pulled my pant legs off, I asked, "Why did you break up?"

He shrugged and pulled the pajama pants off the armrest. "We grew apart."

"Underwear," I interjected.

He raised his eyebrows.

"I need my underwear off. I don't like sleeping with them on."

Figuring this would be the time he would try and get frisky with me, I waited for him to hit on me.

But instead, he continued answering my question as he finished undressing me. "I always talked about moving back to Minnesota, and my ex made it clear she was never moving from Indiana. I think with that in the back of our minds, we slowly pulled away from one another until, one day, we were like, *Why are we still together?*"

"So, it was mutual?"

"Yep. We're still friends. I even introduced her to her fiancé. Go figure."

Sebastian helped me get my pants on, and without thinking, I ran my fingers through his hair. It was softer than it looked.

He lifted his eyes to mine.

I wanted to kiss him. I wanted to do a lot more than that.

He took my hand in his and kissed my palm. "Are you hungry? I can make something or go pick some food up."

"I'm not really that hungry."

"How about soup then? You should try and eat a little before bed."

Soup didn't sound half bad.

"Bad news: I don't think I have any." With always being on the go, I was horrible about grocery shopping.

"I'll run to the store and buy some. Or would you prefer a restaurant?"

"Store is fine."

Sebastian stood and grabbed his keys. "Any favorites or anything you don't like?"

"I'll eat whatever."

"Is there anything I can get you before I go?"

I looked around. "The remote? A glass of water?"

He handed me the remote, which had been over by the TV, and went to get me a glass of water.

I had to say, having someone take care of me felt pretty nice.

Turning on the television, I found a rerun of a popular comedy, and Sebastian brought me water.

He kissed me on the head. "I'll be right back."

"Okay," I said and lay back in my chair. "I'll be here."

Chapter Twen-y-Seven

PRU

THE ROOM WAS DARK, and I was on my back. Instantly, I called out Sebastian's name.

When a light in the hallway flicked on and he appeared in my doorway, I wasn't quite prepared for the level of relief I felt.

"Are you okay?" he asked, his voice full of concern as he walked over to me. "Do you need a pain med? You were due for another one, but I didn't want to wake you."

I didn't feel that bad at the moment, but I knew it was wiser to keep up on my medication instead of waiting for the pain to kick in because then it could be harder to get the pain back under control.

"I can get it," I said, pushing myself up.

"Don't even think about it," he said with a nudge to my shoulder. "I'll be right back."

Less than a minute later, he was back with two pills

and water. After taking them, I was worried that he would leave.

"Are you hungry?"

"Did you get the soup?" The last thing I remembered was him leaving for the store.

"Yes. But you were sleeping in your chair when I got home. I didn't want to wake you, so I carried you to bed. I can make you something to eat if you'd like?"

I checked the clock. It was after eleven. I didn't want to eat now.

"Will you lie with me?" I asked.

I couldn't read his facial expression well because the light from the hall was behind him and my room was still dark.

When he didn't answer right away, I actually got nervous. But I also realized he might want to sleep in his own bed. "It's okay. You don't have to. I'm sure you want to get home."

Sebastian sighed and turned around.

I frowned in confusion. I didn't think he would just leave like that without a word.

But when the light went out in the hallway, I understood that he was shutting off everything before he came back to me.

"What were you doing before I woke up?" I asked when he returned.

He walked around to the other side of the bed. "Watching TV."

"Did I interrupt something good?"

"You could never interrupt me, Pru." He dropped down on top of the comforter and moaned. "Oh God."

I smiled. "Feel good?"

"Yes. Your couch isn't the most comfortable."

"That's because I bought it for looks, not for comfort." And I had spent a nice amount of money on my mattress.

He turned his head. "That's crazy talk." He laid an arm out and patted his chest. "Come over here."

"Get under the covers, Sebastian. It's late. Then, I'll come over there."

I could barely make out the grin on his face. "For someone who *asked me* to lie with her, you sure are bossy."

I shoved his side. "Just do it."

"The thing is, I can't sleep in my jeans. Or my shirt. And I don't want you to think I'm putting moves on you."

"That didn't even cross my mind." I wanted to feel his skin against my cheek anyway.

He rolled off the mattress, stripped out of his clothes, and slipped in beside me. I scooted closer, but mostly, he came to me, and I rested my head on his shoulder.

I sighed with contentment.

"Wake me when you're in pain again, okay? You don't need to get up."

I ran my hand down his chest but stopped when I got to his treasure trail and slipped it around his waist. I wasn't about to tease him and leave him hanging.

"Okay," I agreed.

He kissed the top of my head. "Night, Pru. Don't forget to wake me."

I shifted my head and kissed his neck, lingering there so I could breathe in his scent. "I won't," I whispered, but I thought he had already fallen asleep.

———

It was barely dawn when I did finally wake, and the first thing I did was assess my body. I was still lying on Sebastian. I couldn't believe I had stayed there all night.

It had to be my meds.

But I could worry about that later, seeing as the thing that was causing the most pain was my bladder.

I carefully slid off Sebastian's shoulder and arm. I could tell that I was still sore from yesterday, but now, I was also stiff. My bathroom had never felt so far away.

Despite knowing I could wake Sebastian for help, I was determined to do it myself. He was going to go home eventually, and I couldn't expect him to take care of me. I wasn't his girlfriend. We were barely friends. I needed to do this alone.

It took some time, especially since I was trying not to wake him, but I did it. Once I was upright, it was easier for me to move. My legs were also tight, but the ER physician had warned me that would happen because I had tensed up, bracing for impact, and now, my muscles were rebelling.

Even though I had to empty my bladder, I went for my ibuprofen first. Since I had gone the rest of the night without my prescription, I was hoping to stay off of the pain pills. I didn't want to sleep all day.

I popped some pills in my mouth, used the bathroom, and brushed my teeth. I was feeling better and even thought about taking a shower, but my stomach rumbled, reminding me I hadn't had dinner last night.

But when I opened the door to go search for food, I was frightened to death by the brooding, half-naked male lurking outside the bathroom.

With one arm propped up on the frame, he practically growled, "What the hell are you doing?"

"I was peeing," I told him bluntly. "What are you doing, besides scaring me?"

He grunted. "You were supposed to wake me."

"It's not the middle of the night," I pointed out.

He stepped closer. "If you weren't hurt..."

I tilted my head to the side. "You'd what?" I taunted.

He smiled, as if he'd thought of some inside joke. "I'd fuck you until your pussy was sore."

God. I wanted that too. "So, what are you going to do instead?"

My stomach growled, and Sebastian laughed.

"Looks like I'm going to feed you," he said.

"Not as much fun." I kissed his chest. "But I like that idea."

He groaned and spun away from me. "Life is not fair," he muttered to himself. He turned back in my direction. "Come on, Pru. Let's find you some food."

Chapter Twenty-Eight

SEBASTIAN

"*UGH,*" Pru exclaimed so loud that it came through the bathroom door, followed by the sound of a bottle hitting the shower floor.

I knocked and opened the door. "Are you okay?"

"No," she said, clearly pissed off. "It hurts to lift my arms, and...I just want to feel clean after the accident and being at the hospital."

I wasn't too surprised that she was struggling. I had needed to help her put her braids up in a ponytail and then wrap them into a bun on the top of her head before she got under the water.

"Can I assist you?" I asked.

"I don't know how—unless you get in here with me," she said with a light laugh.

I stripped off my clothes and pulled the curtain to the side, and Pru spun around.

"That's exactly what I was thinking." I held out my hand. "Hand me the soap."

"I don't use soap. I use body wash." She scanned my body and stopped at my hardening dick. "And I'm not sure you should be in here with that thing."

"I don't have complete control over him. And when I see a beautiful, naked woman, he has a tendency to react. I can restrain myself."

Pru smiled and stepped closer. "What if I can't?" As she wrapped her hand around my cock, she kissed me.

I knew she was too sore for sex, but I closed my eyes and gave in for a moment. I cupped the back of her head with my hands and kissed her back. She stroked my length as I explored her mouth.

When I was ready to push her against the side of the shower, I knew it was time to stop. I stepped back, breathing heavily, and turned my eyes to the ceiling. "This might have been a bad idea."

She chuckled and kissed my chin. "I'll stop because as much as I want to have sex with you, I don't think I could handle it."

"Does this mean you're going to let go of my dick?"

Immediately, her hand vanished. "Oops. My bad," she said a little too sweetly.

I looked down at her. "I don't believe you."

Pru handed me a loofah full of suds. "Here's the body wash. I already did my front, but I couldn't get my back or my legs. It hurts to bend over."

"Lift your chin."

She did, and I ran the loofah over her upper chest and shoulders.

"Even if you already did it, I don't do a half-assed job," I told her, lathering both arms.

"I'm not complaining." She closed her eyes as the corners of her mouth tugged upward.

I soaped up her abdomen and came back up to her breasts. I teased the rough edges of the loofah on her nipples until they were hard peaks and gently pinched one between my thumb and finger. "Just making sure they're clean," I told her.

I knelt down and washed the front of each leg, going up and down several times until I had scrubbed every inch of her skin, down to the tips of her toes.

"Turn around," I said in a rough voice.

Once her back was to me, I cleaned the backs of her legs the same way I had the front. Before I took care her full ass, I planted a peck on one cheek and nipped the other. Pru made a small noise but didn't move away.

I washed her butt, taking more time than I needed, and stood to finish her back. By the time I reached the top of her shoulders, where I had started, she was breathing hard, and her eyes were still closed.

Finding a hook on her shower caddy, I hung up the loofah and grabbed her detachable showerhead. I rinsed her off, making sure I got all the soap off her. When I finished, I hung it up and pulled her body back against mine.

"I think I missed a spot," I said next to her ear.

She sucked in a breath as I glided my hand between her legs. I went immediately for her hard nub and rubbed.

Pru moaned and clutched my forearm.

"Let me know if you want me to stop."

"Don't you dare," she said as her hips rotated and her ass hit my cock.

I rubbed her clit until her chest heaved, and I was almost completely holding her up. "Let go, Pru."

She exploded in my arms, knees buckling as she cried out in pleasure.

At this point, my dick ached, but it was worth it to make Pru come.

When she blinked up at me, I said, "All clean."

She grinned at me and pulled my head down for a kiss. "Thank you."

"You're welcome. You deserved it."

She turned in my arms and grasped my shaft once again. "Your turn."

Wrapping my fingers around her wrist, I said, "I didn't do that for you, so you would do it back to me."

"I know. That's why you deserve this too."

I hesitated out of guilt.

"Sebastian?"

"Yeah."

"I want to do this. Let me do this for you."

Slowly, I let go and let her touch me. I closed my eyes, so I could enjoy her touch, but I came almost embarrassingly fast. When I opened my eyes, Pru stared in amazement as she licked my cum off her finger.

"I knew you'd taste good."

"Goddamn." I hauled her into my arms. "I can't wait to be inside you again."

PRU

"WE'RE HERE," a voice yelled from the front of my house.

"Coming," I called back from my bedroom.

It was Wednesday night, and my friends and I were supposed to go out to dinner, but they were all coming to my house instead. It had been five days since the accident, and while I was feeling better, my friends had insisted that we hang out at home rather than go to a restaurant.

But even though we weren't going out, I'd put on jeans, a sweater, and makeup. I'd been wearing loungewear for almost a week, so it felt nice to put on something else and to make myself look pretty.

I left my bedroom to see all six of my friends had arrived.

"Did you all drive together?" I asked.

"I picked up Bree," Tessa said.

"I came with Elizabeth," Isabelle said.

"We came in our own cars," Paisley said, pointing to

herself and Alexis with her thumb. "We have really good timing, is all."

"She said six o'clock," Tessa said. "And it's five after."

"That I did," I said, looking at what she held in her hand. "What did you bring?"

She lifted what looked like a wine bottle. "Sparkling grape juice for Alexis and me. And you, if you need some."

"I brought wine," Bree said, waving her own bottle around.

"I can have one glass," I said. I wasn't taking my prescription pain meds anymore, but I didn't want to drink too much in case something happened and I needed them. "And I ordered the pizzas," I said. "Let's go get some glasses."

"Where did you order from?" Alexis asked as we headed toward my kitchen.

"My favorite restaurant."

"They deliver now?" Tessa asked.

"No. I have someone bringing it to me." Opening the cupboard, I began to pull out wineglasses for everyone.

"What app do you use?" Bree asked. "There are so many. DoorDash, Grubhub, Uber Eats, and I'm sure there are more. I haven't signed up for any because I don't know which one is the best."

"I don't use any of those apps. At least, not yet." I might have to sign up for one though. I still didn't have a car because I was waiting for insurance.

Alexis looked around. "Is that your garage door?"

Everyone quieted, and I listened to the hum of the big

double door going up. The sound stopped for ten seconds and started again, indicating it was going back down.

"Yep. Pizza is here." I rubbed my hands together. "I can't wait."

My friends were all watching me with confused looks. "What?"

But none of them had the chance to answer because the door to the house opened, and Sebastian walked into the kitchen with three large pizza boxes. "Dinner is served," he said setting two down in front of me and one off to the side.

"Thanks, Sebastian," I said, opening the first box and moving it to the right side of the counter. "Do you want some?" I turned around to see he was gone. "Where did he go?"

Six sets of eyes stared at me.

"What is with the looks tonight?"

Bree stepped forward and lowered her voice. "Sebastian is here."

Was that a statement or a question? "Yes. And?"

"I thought you hated him?" Tessa asked.

"I don't hate him."

Paisley snorted. "Well, you sure didn't like him at our last dinner together."

I lifted a shoulder. "I've gotten to know him better. He's not that bad."

"That still doesn't explain what he's doing here. Tonight," Bree said.

"*Oh,*" I said in realization. I'd thought she already

knew this because I assumed Sebastian had told her. Plus, he had been here the day of my accident. "He's been helping me out. I don't have a car yet, and I'm not really fit to drive yet anyway."

Alexis pointed down. "So, he's been staying here? Or does he go home every night?"

"He's been staying here."

Alexis looked at everyone but me. "She says it like it's no big deal."

"Because it's not—"

"Pru?"

We all turned as Sebastian walked back into the kitchen, wearing a white T-shirt and gray sweatpants. He put them on almost every night after work, and I loved those sweatpants. I had taken back everything bad I'd thought about gray sweats. It was nice to have my own personal eye candy.

Paisley must have agreed because she reached out and gripped my arm as she made a low-pitched squeal through her closed mouth.

"Yeah?" I answered him.

"I'll be downstairs, so I don't bug you ladies."

"Do you want to take some pizza?"

"Nah." He picked up the box he had set aside. "I got my own. But thank you." He headed for the stairs.

"Don't forget napkins."

He raised his hand and waved some back and forth. "I already grabbed some."

The sound of footsteps heading to the lower level

reverberated through the house, and once again, my friends all turned to me.

"Are you two dating?" Isabelle asked.

"No."

"*Pru,*" Paisley said, emphasizing my name. "Please tell me you're having sex with him at least." She swung her head around to everyone. "You all saw what he was packing in his sweatpants, right?"

She got several nods in return.

I plucked her hand off my arm. "Yes and no to the sex question. We have slept together in the past, but we haven't done so since my accident."

Despite hints that I wanted to have sex, Sebastian didn't want to hurt me. He was sweet but frustrating.

Bree dropped her chin. "But you're not dating."

I laughed at her expression. "No. We're friends. He's helping me out."

"Where is he sleeping?" Tessa asked, arms crossed over her chest.

Pausing, I tried to think of a good way to explain this, but I couldn't. They wouldn't understand how he comforted me at night.

"With me," I admitted.

Bree threw up her hands, Paisley wiggled her eyebrows, and Tessa dropped her arms.

"I knew it," Paisley said.

"Can we just eat pizza and hang out, please? Otherwise, I'll have Sebastian come up here and kick you all out."

"He's your bodyguard," Elizabeth said. "I got it."

She was the one I had told the most to, so I smiled at her in appreciation. "Exactly."

Alexis grinned at me. "Look at her. Pretending that she doesn't have feelings when we all know they're going to end up together."

"Pfft. No, we won't."

Everyone laughed, except Bree.

When I met her eyes, she pointed two fingers at her eyes and then one at me.

I waved her off. She could watch me all she wanted; nothing was going to happen.

Chapter Thirty

SEBASTIAN

SATURDAY MORNING, I had to drag my ass out of bed because I had to get to work since I had missed last weekend, but I was tired.

Yesterday had marked a week since Pru's accident, and I'd finally given in to both our desires and had sex with her. But since I was still worried about hurting her, I insisted she be on top. That might have been a mistake.

She rode me hard until we both came, stripped off the condom, put on a new one, and rode me again. For someone who had been in a car wreck a week ago, she sure had a lot of stamina. And after we'd finished, I was pretty sure I had been more worn out than she was.

But then again, she didn't have to get up for work this morning.

I kissed Pru on the forehead. "I'm going to work. Have a good day."

She brushed her lips against mine, muttered, "You too," and pulled her covers up over half her head.

After grabbing my mug of coffee, I headed to work. I'd just pulled out of the driveway when my phone rang. I answered through my car's Bluetooth.

"Good morning, Bree."

"Good morning. I'm surprised you're up this early. I was going to leave you a voice mail."

"I'm on my way to work. What are you doing awake?"

She sighed. "Last-minute wedding planning."

"And let me guess. That's why you called me?"

"You're so smart."

I laughed. "What do you want?"

She scoffed. "Who? Me?"

"Bree."

"I'm kidding. I'm calling because your tux is finally in for the wedding. Are you able to pick it up soon?"

"Ohh. I work all weekend. Can you pick it up for me, and I'll get it from you?"

"No, because you have to try it on and make sure it fits."

"Shit. That's right."

"They're open late on Saturdays. You can probably go after work."

Pru and I were supposed to hang out after I got off, so I didn't really want to waste time picking up my tux, but I would do it for my cousin.

"Do you have plans?" Bree asked.

"Yes, but I can put it off for an hour or however long it takes."

"Are your plans with a certain woman whose name starts with a *P*?"

I chuckled. "Yes."

"Are you still staying with her?"

"I am. She still doesn't have a car, and I like helping her out."

"And you like having sex with her?"

"That's nice too."

"Look, Sebastian—"

"Bree," I cut her off. "I'm not going to hurt Pru, if that's what you're worried about. I like her."

"While I appreciate that, I'm worried that she's going to be the one to hurt you."

Laughing, I said, "Me?"

"Yes. What, are you immune to feelings or something?"

"You know I'm not, but I'm also not worried about Pru hurting me. It's not like she's using me or anything. She didn't even ask me for help. I insisted on it."

"No, I don't think she's using you. I genuinely think she likes you too."

Hearing this put a grin on my face.

"I'm just worried that you might get more serious than her and things won't end well."

"Thank you for the concern, but I'll be fine."

"I'm sure you will. Just be cautious, okay?"

"For you, I will."

"Thank you." She sounded relieved. "And thank you for picking up your tux tonight."

"You're welcome. The day is coming soon, and I want to be ready as much as I can."

"You're the *best* best man I could ask for."

"I'm more than happy to do this."

"Call me if you need any help with the tux."

"Will do."

"Later, coz."

I smiled. "Later."

———

A couple hours later, I called Pru.

"Hello?"

"Hey, I know we have plans tonight, but I won't be home right away after work."

"Okay. What's going on?"

"I have a date with another woman. I forgot about it. She asked me a couple of weeks ago, and I feel awful, telling her no at the last minute."

"Really?"

I leaned back in my chair. "That's not going to be a problem, is it? We're not official, are we?"

"No, it's fine."

I was completely teasing about the date, and I wasn't hiding it. I was sure Pru could hear it in the tone of my voice, and her response was fitting for her, giving me as much shit back as I was giving her, but Bree's words echoed through my brain.

I was suddenly mad at myself for starting the joke in the first place. I needed to finish it.

"Should I tell her you said hi? Or do you want to join us? Threesome?"

"She can join us, but she'll be watching in the corner while you fuck me. Then, she can go on her merry little way, knowing she'll never be as lucky as me."

I burst out laughing, and any concern I might have had from Bree's comments melted away.

"Damn, woman, you're making me hard, and I'm at work."

"Serves you right."

"Yeah, you're probably right."

"What are you really doing tonight?"

"I have to go and try on my tux for the wedding."

"Oh, fun."

Hmm. "Do you want to come with? Or are you joking? I don't think it will actually be fun."

"Sebastian, I've barely gone anywhere in a week. I would *love* to go."

"I'll pick you up after work then."

"I'll be ready."

"Except you're not supposed to see me in my tuxedo until I'm walking down the aisle." For some reason, I felt the need to throw one more joke in there. "Oh, wait. That's the bride and her wedding dress. I guess you can see me and all my handsomeness."

"I'd better get to see you because you and I are not getting married."

I rubbed my chest. We hadn't known each other long, and she could mean we weren't getting married *right now* or *yet*. But the tightness I felt under my sternum told me I could be fooling myself.

Chapter Thirty-One

PRU

I WAS ENJOYING the taste of Sebastian's hard cock in my mouth when I was yanked off of him and thrown on the bed.

I frowned at him. "What are you doing?"

Sebastian moved between my legs and pushed my thighs wide. "I don't want to come in your mouth. I want to come in your pussy."

"Your dirty mouth shouldn't turn me on so much, but it does."

The corner of his mouth went up in a smirk. "I'd better check." He sucked on his first two fingers and then slowly pushed them inside me. "Fuck yes." He yanked his hand away, placed his dick at my entrance, and thrust inside.

We both groaned.

"Goddamn, you feel amazing."

It had been a month or so since my accident, and while Sebastian didn't stay with me every night, we were sleeping together on the regular. And we had both recently agreed to give up condoms. I thought we'd had sex almost every night since then.

"So do you," I told him. "Now, move. We have a wedding to get to."

Sebastian grinned down at me and began to pump his hips.

———

When Sebastian and I got to the church, we found Bree pacing.

"Oh, thank God you're here," she said when she saw me.

"What's wrong?"

"Tessa."

I gasped. "Is she okay?"

"She is as long as she's sitting or lying down. She didn't feel good in the middle of the night, so Seth took her to the hospital, and the doctor suspected preeclampsia. She's supposed to follow up with her OB." Bree rubbed her forehead. "Whenever she stands up, her blood pressure skyrockets, so even if it's not preeclampsia, she can't be my matron of honor today."

I grabbed Bree's hands and forced her to look at me. "What can I do?"

"You can be my maid of honor."

"Me?"

"You're one of my closest friends, and I would love for

you to step in. And I figured since you were at the rehearsal last night, you know where to stand and what Tessa was supposed to do. Plus, you've attended more weddings for your job than all of us combined. I was hoping that would make the last-minute change less stressful for you."

Being a part of the wedding was a lot different than planning it. And I had already had to psych myself up to come to the wedding with Sebastian. And now, she wanted me to be the maid of honor to his best man.

"Are you sure you don't want someone else?" I practically begged.

"No, I want you."

I took a deep breath, knowing I couldn't leave Bree hanging. "Okay, put me to work."

———

Bree and Tessa had picked an empire waist dress since they hadn't known how big her pregnant belly would be, so I was able to wear it pretty easily.

And when I slipped my arm into Sebastian's and he smiled down at me, I got a funny feeling in my stomach. Walking down the aisle with him in a church while everyone stared at us was not what I'd pictured happening today, but it actually went fast. And when Bree walked in, all eyes turned to her. I was still relieved when it was over.

"Are you doing okay?" Sebastian asked after he walked me back down the aisle.

"Yes, but I did learn that from now on, maybe I should be kinder to my wedding party members when they panic."

"Wait." He chuckled. "Are you saying you've never been in a wedding before?"

"I haven't. Everyone wants me to plan it instead."

"That's not fair."

"It's fine. I'd rather be in the back, telling everyone what to do."

He laughed. "You?" he joked.

I smacked his arm.

"I suppose it was good practice because someday, you'll have your own wedding. You can't have anyone else take your place as the bride."

I smiled awkwardly as I studied his face. I hoped that he didn't think we were going to get married. I drew my arm away from his.

Sebastian frowned. "What's wrong?"

"Nothing," I lied. "I think I need some air."

"I'll go with you."

I put my hand up. "No, because I need to go to the restroom first," I lied again.

"I understand. Don't be too long though. We're going to the reception in a limo."

I smiled reassuringly. "I'll be back."

———

At the reception, all my friends made sure to tell me how good I looked with Sebastian.

"Thanks, but can we focus on Bree and Zack? It's their wedding." Really, I didn't want any more comments about Sebastian and me. I was beginning to feel like I couldn't breathe.

"They already know they look good," Paisley said.

"It would still be nice to hear since I'm the bride and all," Bree said, hands on her hips.

"You're a beautiful bride," Tessa said from her seat at a table. Since the doctor had said she had to be sitting, she had insisted on coming and parked herself at a table. Luckily, she had her husband ready to get her anything she needed.

"Thank you," Bree said to her new sister-in-law.

Out of the corner of my eye, I watched Sebastian approach us.

"Good evening, ladies. Do you mind if I steal Pru for a dance?"

Paisley grinned. "Be our guest."

I let Sebastian drag me away, but all I could think was that everyone was going to be watching us the whole time. But if I'd told Sebastian no, I would have been stuck, listening to my friends talk about us. When an older couple interrupted us on our way, I was so relieved even though I had no idea who they were.

"Sebastian, introduce us," the woman said.

Alarm bells went off. That was an all-too-familiar tone she had taken with him.

"Mom, Dad, this is Pru."

His mom smiled. "Hello, Pru. How do you know Sebastian?"

"Mom." Sebastian's tone came off as a warning, but he was grinning.

He was enjoying this, but I was freaking out. He'd never told me his parents were going to be here. I realized I should have known, seeing as Bree was his cousin, but he still could have warned me. I felt like I was being ambushed.

"Ignore him, dear," his mom said.

"I'm sorry, what was the question?"

"How do you know Sebastian?" She looked down to where my hand was in his.

I gently pulled mine away. "Oh, I've been friends with Bree since high school. And I'm the one planning Sebastian's fundraiser for his fire department."

The three of them stared at me as if they were waiting for me to say something else, but I couldn't.

"Excuse me," I said and ran toward a door to find someplace to hide.

Chapter Thirty-Two

SEBASTIAN

"WHAT JUST HAPPENED?" my dad asked.

I smiled politely at my parents. "Let me go see if Pru's all right. We'll talk later?"

"Yes," my mom said, patting the top of my hand.

I didn't have a good feeling as I went to look for Pru. Despite her telling me that we weren't getting married that day I'd picked up my tuxedo for the wedding, I'd figured she had meant at that moment in time.

Things had been good for us since then. I did try to make sure I gave her enough space and didn't pressure her too much, and I'd thought going to Bree and Zack's wedding together was a good sign.

Apparently, I was wrong.

I found her outside, sitting on the stairs. "Pru?" I said, warning her before I sat down beside her.

She rubbed the back of her neck. "I was pretty rude back there, wasn't I? I'm sorry."

"What happened?"

"I don't know."

"Did you get scared?"

She chuckled. "I suppose I did."

"Can I ask you a question?"

"Always."

Somehow, I doubted that.

"Is the thought of being in a relationship with me so bad?"

She turned to me and put her hand on my arm. "What? No. No, it's not. You're a great guy, Sebastian."

"But?"

"But nothing. It's the truth."

"Okay, so why did you tell my parents that you are Bree's friend and my event planner?"

She shrugged. "I don't know. I panicked."

"So, I'm a great guy, and the thought of being in a relationship with me isn't bad, but actually being in a relationship with me is not good?"

"I didn't say that."

It was beginning to look like Bree had been right.

"You and I have been together since your accident. I was practically living at your house for a while. Shit, we even decided that we were only fucking each other." Foolish me had mistaken that for commitment. "But you can't say you're dating me. You can't admit that you're my girlfriend."

She winced, and it was all the answer I needed.

"Wow." I threw her hand off my arm and stood. "And

to think, I was actually considering myself your boyfriend."
I shook my head back and forth. "I should have known."

"Should have known what?" she asked, her eyes narrowing to bore a hole into me.

I pointed a finger. "Oh, no, you don't get to be mad at me."

She jumped off the stairs. "I don't? I didn't want to be in a relationship, Sebastian. I didn't want to get involved with you. I thought I'd made that pretty clear."

"Excuse me for liking you. And I don't remember you kicking me out of your life. In fact, if I recall, you're the one who invited me back into your bed."

"To *sleep*. Not for sex."

I raised my hands in frustration. "Are you serious? You asked me to lay with you when you were hurt and vulnerable. That sounds way more like you like me than just asking me to fuck your brains out."

She licked her lips, and for a moment, I had a hope that she saw where I was coming from.

"Can you just tell me one thing?"

"What?"

"We don't have to tell anyone else. We don't have to admit anything to anyone. But will you at least tell me that things are serious between us? That we are in a relationship?"

"I..."

I waited longer than I should have for her to tell me what I wanted to hear. But after several seconds, I knew I was in denial.

"That's what I thought." I turned on my heel and forced myself to go back to the party.

I heard a little later that Pru had left, telling everyone she wasn't feeling well. I heard one of her friends joke that she was the next one pregnant, and I pictured for a minute that she was. I didn't even want to think of the ways she'd keep me out of her life if we shared a child.

I made it through the rest of the reception and went home alone.

The next day, I messaged Pru to tell her I'd be over to talk to her. I thought maybe after a night to cool off, we'd do better, trying to have a civil conversation. But when I got there, she was gone.

It was all I needed to know.

I packed up my stuff, left her house key and her garage door opener, and walked out the door.

I really hated that things had ended this way, but I told myself it was better to get hurt now than later.

Chapter Thirty-Three

PRU

One Month Later

I TOOK a sip of my wine and looked at Bree. "I know you didn't ask me to brunch for just any reason."

She chuckled. "Am I that obvious?"

"Yes." I smiled, looking down at the napkin she couldn't stop fiddling with. "But maybe it's because I've known you for a long time."

"Tonight is the fundraiser, right?"

Oof. This was a hard topic. "It is. Why?"

"Are you still the head planner? Will you be there?"

"I will. Just because things ended with Sebastian and me doesn't mean I'd give the event to someone else."

In truth, this event was what had been holding me together. I hadn't seen Sebastian since the night of Bree's wedding, and I missed him something awful. I thought maybe if I saw him one more time, it would remind me that we were better off apart, but really, I just wanted to see him again.

"I figured you wouldn't. That's why I wanted to meet with you."

I swallowed. I had a feeling that I wasn't going to like what she had to say. I straightened my spine and tried to give off the impression I wasn't worried. "What's going on?"

"I just thought you should know that Sebastian is seeing someone else."

My breathing got tight, and I felt like I'd been punched in the chest. "Oh. I guess that doesn't surprise me. He's a good-looking guy."

Bree tilted her head to the side. "Pru, you don't have to act tough with me. I know you liked him."

I shook my head. "I'm not being tough. It was bound to happen." I shoved my chair back from the table and stood. Plastering a fake smile on my face, I said, "Speaking of the fundraiser, I need to get going. I have plenty to do before the event starts."

"Pru, please don't leave."

Swinging my purse onto my arm, I waved at Bree with way more enthusiasm than was called for. "I gotta go. Later."

I ran to my car, and it wasn't until I got there that I realized I hadn't paid my bill. But I couldn't go back now because before I was even out of the parking lot, I had started to cry.

———

It had been hard, but I had managed to compose myself. I had let myself cry all the way home, but once I was there, I'd commanded myself to get it together. Knowing he had already moved on told me I had been right about him all along. Alpha males didn't need someone when there was always a new person to take that someone's place, and I could not let Sebastian see me a mess, especially now that I knew he had someone else in his life.

I rubbed my knuckles over my sternum as I watched the first guests of the night walk in. They were dressed nice and looked happy to be at the event. I just hoped they were ready to spend some money, so this event would be a smashing success.

Ten minutes later, I watched as Sebastian walked through the doors, and I sucked in a breath. We had decided to have the firefighters wear their uniforms rather than dress up because people liked to see them dressed like that. I was one of them. Sebastian looked so happy, and when he laughed at something another coworker had said, it made my heart skip a beat.

I was so invested in him that I almost forgot to look for the new woman he was seeing. I scanned every face around him, but no one seemed to be with him, which made sense because he had walked in with his coworkers. It looked like I was going to have to wait to see his new girlfriend.

More guests arrived, and soon, I was pulled away from

Sebastian and back to my job. Thankfully, it did distract me for some time, and I got caught up in a catering mishap that I had to help smooth out, but soon, dinner was served, and no one was the wiser.

I was making sure all the food was being cleaned up when the DJ approached me.

"Pru?"

"Yeah," I said, spinning around.

"It's time for the auction. Do you need me to wait?"

I looked back and forth between the catering team and the DJ. The catering team was almost finished, and I knew they could handle it.

"No, I'm ready."

I followed the DJ back to the front of the room and took my spot behind his booth off to the side of the stage, where I had a decent view. The DJ was going to be the MC for the event, and I was going to keep track of everyone who won their bids on each firefighter. I needed to make sure the money got paid and that the firefighter and their dinner date met up later.

The DJ hopped up onto the stage, and the crowd started to quiet. But it wasn't until he tapped the microphone and said, "Attention, ladies and gentlemen," that everyone hushed. The DJ proceeded to welcome the guests and to explain what the auction was and how it worked.

I found Sebastian in the crowd, sitting next to Rory. There was a woman sitting next to him, but he didn't seem to be talking to her. I had no idea if this was who he was with or if she was there with someone else, and I hated that I wanted to know.

I must have stared a little too long because Sebastian suddenly stiffened and his eyes went in my direction. I looked down as soon as he spotted me.

"Wuss," I said to myself, and because I was worried he was still watching me, I studied the list of firefighter names on the clipboard in front of me.

Sebastian's name was at the end. Just like mine had been.

Fuck, Pru, do not think about the night of your auction.

Quickly, I turned my attention to the DJ and forced myself to listen to him. And after what felt like forever, he called up the first firefighter.

———

I marked down another amount next to a name and had to smile. It was Rory, and it seemed like he was going on a date with someone who would be perfect for him.

But happiness was replaced with nervousness because there was only one name left.

"Ladies and gentlemen, our last firefighter of the night is Sebastian Creed. He was born and raised in Minnesota. He moved away for a number of years and came back to the area less than a year ago. He is the person who helped plan this wonderful event, and from what I heard, he dragged his feet at the thought of being bid on. So, what do you say? Let's give Sebastian a warm applause and show him that this auction is a great time."

Sebastian stood and waved to the crowd. There were a lot of yells and even some whistles as he made his way to the stage. My eyes scanned the audience to see who would be bidding on him.

The DJ lowered his hands, and the cheering quieted. "Is everyone ready? Let's start the bidding at—"

"One hundred dollars," a woman yelled.

The DJ looked impressed. "Okay. We'll start at one hundred dollars."

I squinted my eyes, trying to see the woman better. *Is this who Bree was talking about?*

"Two hundred," a different woman said.

"Three hundred," another one said.

Three women? How was I ever going to figure out who his new girlfriend was?

My head felt like a volleyball as I watched the three ladies go back and forth on their bids, and I felt like the walls were closing in on me as the price went higher and higher.

For some reason, I felt a pull to look at Sebastian, and when I did, I was shocked to see his eyes were on me.

He raised his eyebrows at me, and before I knew it, I stepped around the booth and yelled, "Five thousand dollars."

There were several audible gasps, and the crowd hushed as everyone gawked at me. Sebastian leaned toward the DJ and whispered in the man's ear.

The DJ frowned but raised the mic to his mouth. "Sebastian has asked for a quick time-out."

Sebastian smiled and held up one finger, as if to say he'd be right back, but when I realized half the eyes were still on me, I went back behind the booth and tried to hide. It was pointless because he followed me there.

"What are you doing, Pru?" he asked, his face serious.

"My job," I said, clearly ignoring his real question.

His brown eyes sparkled with amusement. "You know what I mean. Why are you bidding on me? You know you can have me for free."

His new lady would probably disagree with his statement.

"Could have had," I corrected.

His brow furrowed. "What do you mean?"

"You said I can have you for free. You meant, *could have had*—past tense."

"Ahh. So, why did you bid on me?"

I stared over his shoulder. "I don't know."

He growled, and with wide eyes, I turned back to him.

His face was stern. "Please stop with *I don't know*. Just tell me what you want."

"You, okay? I want you. I was scared. I was worried you'd move on from me, so I pushed you away first. I made a mistake. I want to give us a chance. I want to be with you. And I don't want anyone else to bid on you."

A slow smile spread across his face. "Okay."

"Okay?"

"Okay."

"What does that even mean?"

"It means, if you're serious, I'm yours. Besides, you still owe me a date, babe."

I ignored his joke. "What about the new woman you're seeing?"

He frowned and shook his head. "I'm not dating anyone."

I pursed my lips. "*Bree*," I said, cursing her name. She'd lied to me. She was getting an earful from me later.

"Bree? What about her?"

"Never mind." I glanced at the crowd, who was starting to get antsy. "You'd better go back up there."

He stepped closer, wrapping an arm around my waist and yanking me to him. With his mouth against my ear, he said, "If you do this, I'm taking you home and fucking you tonight, and I'm never leaving."

I closed my eyes, remembering similar words he had spoken to me all those weeks ago.

"Yes or no, Pru? Are you going to be mine? Forever this time?"

If I let myself answer honestly, it was what I truly wanted, and I would be a fool to deny the two of us any longer.

Wrapping my arms around his neck, I nodded. "Yes," I whispered back. "I love you."

"Hallelujah. Because I love you too." He kissed my neck and stepped back. "Now, I'd better get my ass back up there, so you can claim it as yours."

Epilogue

PRU

MY FRIENDS and I raised our glasses and clinked them together. "Cheers," we all said around the table.

"To the last United She-Woman Single Ladies with Our Vibrators So We Never Have Another Bad Date or Experience Romance Again Because Men Suck Club dinner," I said.

"What are you talking about?" Bree said.

I laughed and set my wine down. "Come on. Three of us are married. Two of us are living with our boyfriends. And two of us are just starting a relationship." My eyes traveled over to Elizabeth and Isabelle to see if they were okay with what I'd said. I'd told Elizabeth I would open the conversation she'd been wanting to have with the rest of our friends for quite some time.

Bree leaned back. "I can't believe this is coming from you. The woman who refused to meet my aunt and uncle at my wedding, and now, she's living with my cousin."

I put my fingers on my chest. "I admit I made a mistake, and I have met your aunt and uncle."

They had been at the fundraiser, and I had officially introduced myself as Sebastian's girlfriend after the auction.

"Just making sure you don't hurt him," she said.

"He's a big boy. He can take care of himself," I said.

Bree lifted her brow. "You'd be surprised. When those alpha men fall, they fall hard."

I smiled to myself. Didn't I know it? "Sebastian tells me he loves me every night before bed, and I never get tired of hearing it."

"Wait a second," Tessa said.

Thankfully, when she had followed up with her OB, she had been diagnosed with gestational hypertension. So, while she had to be monitored more closely, it wasn't as bad as preeclampsia.

"What's wrong?" Alexis asked.

"What Pru said. Three married, two living with boyfriends, and two starting a relationship. That equals all seven of us. And if Pru and Paisley are living with boyfriends and Bree, Alexis, and I are married..."

All eyes turned to Isabelle and Elizabeth.

"Are you two dating someone that we don't know about?" Tessa asked. "And why does Pru know and no one else?"

Elizabeth looked at Isabelle. "Well, it's because of me. I've been scared to tell you."

Paisley leaned over. "You can tell us anything."

Alexis, Bree, and Tessa nodded.

Elizabeth took a breath so large that her shoulders and chest moved. "I like women. I'm a lesbian."

"Oh, thank God," Paisley said. "I was so worried you were dating a married man and you were a home-wrecker."

I laughed as I made eye contact with Elizabeth. I gave her a look, as if to say, *See, it wasn't so bad.*

"But what about Isabelle?" Paisley asked.

Elizabeth took Isabelle's hand.

"Well, it turns out, I'm in love with Elizabeth," Isabelle said. "Elizabeth has known for some time that she likes women, but I just discovered that I feel the same way." She shrugged. "I'm bi."

Everyone got up and hugged the two women.

"I'm so happy for the both of you," I said.

"I guess this really is the end of the United She-Woman Single Ladies with Our Vibrators So We Never Have Another Bad Date or Experience Romance Again Because Men Suck Club," Bree said.

"Hey, it was fun while it lasted," I said.

"We need a new club name," Paisley said.

"How about Off the Market?" Isabelle said.

"But we were already off the market," Tessa said.

"Good point," Isabelle said.

Alexis tapped her chin. "How about Happily Ever After?" she said and laughed.

Despite her making a joke, I knew that I, like my friends, had found my happily ever after.

Better late than never.

. . .

The End

Turn the page for a sample of

NOT ANOTHER MANWHORE

Not Another Manwhore

ZACK

I took a bite of my sandwich and rested my arms on the side of my work truck bed as I watched an unfamiliar black sedan pull up in front of the house I was working on. I'd been installing electrical work there since six that morning, and I was past due for a break.

My sister had asked where I would be around lunch, but that wasn't her car.

The driver's side opened, and Bree Keller, my sister's friend, got out of the vehicle.

I frowned as she neared, and I stepped away from my truck.

She smiled hesitantly. "Hi, Zack."

"Is everything okay with Tessa?"

Bree tilted her head in question. "Didn't she tell you I was stopping by?"

"No."

"Oh, I thought she told you I was coming."

"She didn't." Bree still hadn't answered my question. "Is Tessa okay?"

"Yes, she's fine."

Now that the worry was gone, curiosity took over, and I wondered why she had come to see me. I eyed Bree from her head to foot.

Back in high school, I had seen her around. She'd been cute back then, but she was two years younger than me, and I'd had plenty of girls my own age to keep me occupied.

Now, she was smoking hot with a rocking body, even wearing what looked to be her work clothes. She was about half a foot shorter than my six-one with light-brown hair and fair skin and a sprinkling of freckles across the bridge of her nose. The other night at the restaurant, she hadn't looked so formal with her dark lipstick, and I could still picture her low-cut shirt, showing off an impressive set of tits.

I resumed my position behind my truck before she saw my dick getting hard. He didn't understand that Bree wasn't there to see him.

"What's up?" I asked, picking up my water bottle and taking a long drink in hopes it would cool me down.

The lip Bree was chewing on slid out of her mouth. "I need a favor."

My eyes widened. "From me?"

Even though she was my sister's friend, I didn't know her that well. We'd gone to different high schools, and I'd moved out as soon as I graduated. The most time I could ever remember spending with her was the afternoon my mom had forced me to drive Tessa and two of her friends to the movies. None of them had said a single word to me the whole time. I didn't think I'd even gotten a thank-you.

Maybe I should tell her she already owes me one.

"Yes, from you." She looked away, and her eyes landed on the back of my truck bed. "You're an electrician, right?"

I sighed. I didn't understand why everyone and their dog thought I should help them with a large discount—or even worse, for free. I didn't mind helping my friends with projects in their houses, but when my friend's neighbor's nephew started coming around, my annoyance began to rise.

The good thing was, my budding erection was gone.

"Are you building or remodeling?" I asked.

Because I loved my sister, I'd give Bree advice, but I wasn't going to work for nothing.

"Huh?"

"Are you building a new house or remodeling an old one?" I said a little slower.

Her forehead wrinkled. "Neither." A second later, the area between her eyebrows smoothed out, and she laughed. "Oh. No, I'm not doing either. My favor has nothing to do with you being an electrician."

Interesting. "Okay then, what can I help you with?"

She opened her mouth, but no words came out.

I lifted my brow in question and shoved my last bite of food in my mouth. "It can't be that bad," I said after I swallowed.

"It's embarrassing."

The plot thickens. "If I promise not to laugh, would that help?"

This made her smile, and I hoped I'd eased her mind a little.

"What are you doing next weekend?"

"Are you asking me out on a date?"

"No. I mean, yes." She sighed. "I mean, it's more complicated than that."

I glanced at my watch. The homeowners weren't around, but I still needed to get back to work. I had plans later that evening, and I wanted to be finished up with the wall I was currently wiring.

"I don't mean to be rude, but I need to get back in there." I jabbed my thumb at the house behind me.

"Right. Yeah, I need to get back to work too. I'm on my lunch break."

"So..." I prompted.

"I need a date to my cousin's wedding so that my mother won't harass me all weekend about why I don't have a boyfriend."

"Uh...listen, Bree, I don't go to weddings with women I'm fucking, much less with someone I'm not."

Wrong impressions were had all around when one went with someone to a wedding. Like thoughts of their own nuptials.

My eye twitched at the thought.

"No, I don't want you to be my real date. I want you to be my fake date."

I hadn't expected that. "You want me to be your fake date?"

"Yes. I just need someone to keep my mother—and the rest of my family—out of my hair, and the only way I'm going to do that is if I bring someone."

I rubbed my chin. "You want me to go with you as your fake date?"

"Fake date. Fake boyfriend."

"Oh, it's boyfriend now?"

"It's whatever I need it to be in order to have a peaceful weekend."

Scratching the back of my head, I said, "I don't know—"

"I'm willing to pay you."

"Hmm..." I shook my head. "Nah."

Panic took over her face. "That's it? Nah. You won't even think about it?"

I laughed. "I meant, nah to you paying me."

She gasped. "Does that mean you'll do it?"

"Yes, but instead of you paying me, I want a favor in return."

"What kind of favor?"

"I'm not sure yet. I'll let you know when I've decided." Another thought crossed my mind. "This arrangement, does it include sex?"

Her mouth dropped open. "What? No."

I lifted a shoulder. "I was just checking. You know, because the dick costs extra. You'd owe me two favors instead of one."

When she stood there, unmoving, I walked over to her and pushed her chin up with a finger.

"Lighten up, Bree; it was a joke. If you're going to be uptight all weekend, then it really will cost you extra."

She scowled. "I'm not uptight," she huffed out.

"I guess we'll have to wait and see about that. What time do you need me on Saturday?"

She giggled awkwardly.

Not a good sign.

"Um, the thing is, it's actually from Thursday to Sunday, and it's out of town."

"Holy shit. Kind of left out some important details, huh?"

"Will you let me pay you now?" She clasped her hands together and begged, "Please don't say no."

"Fine. I'll need to move some stuff around for work, but I can manage it." I pointed my finger at her. "But know this: the favor I'm going to ask will be huge."

About the Author

R.L. Kenderson is two best friends writing under one name.

Renae has always loved reading, and in third grade, she wrote her first poem where she learned she might have a knack for this writing thing. Lara remembers sneaking her grandmother's Harlequin novels when she was probably too young to be reading them, and since then, she knew she wanted to write her own.

When they met in college, they bonded over their love of reading and the TV show *Charmed*. What really spiced up their friendship was when Lara introduced Renae to romance novels. When they discovered their first vampire romance, they knew there would always be a special place in their hearts for paranormal romance. After being unable to find certain storylines and characteristics they wanted to read about in the hundreds of books they consumed, they decided to write their own.

One lives in the Minneapolis-St. Paul area and the other in the Kansas City area where they're a sonographer/stay-at-home mom/wife and pharmacist/mother by day, and together they're a sexy author by night. They communicate through phone, email, and whole lot of messaging.

You can find them at http://www.rlkenderson.com, Facebook, Instagram, TikTok, Twitter, and Goodreads. Join their reader group! Or you can email them at rlkenderson@rlkenderson.com, or sign up for their newsletter. They always love hearing from their readers.